MORRILL ELEMENTARY SCHOOL

34880000802368

W9-ATR-939

2-5

PROPERTY OF
CHICAGO BOARD OF EDUCATION
DONALD L. MORRILL SCHOOL

Fic
Eis
c.1 Eisenberg, Lisa

AUTHOR

Lexie On Her Own

TITLE

DATE LOANED	BORROWER'S NAME	DATE RETURNED
	Cealia Rodriguez	3/4
	Sonny Buchanan	3/4

cl

F	Eisenberg, Lisa
EIS	Lexie on her own

PROPERTY OF
CHICAGO BOARD OF EDUCATION
DONALD L. MORRILL SCHOOL

PROPERTY OF
CHICAGO BOARD OF EDUCATION
DONALD L. MORRILL SCHOOL

Lexie On Her Own

Lexie

On Her Own

LISA EISENBERG

PROPERTY OF
CHICAGO BOARD OF EDUCATION
DONALD L. MORRILL SCHOOL

VIKING

VIKING
Published by the Penguin Group
Viking Penguin, a division of Penguin Books USA Inc.,
375 Hudson Street, New York, New York 10014, U.S.A.
Penguin Books Ltd, 27 Wrights Lane, London W8 5TZ, England
Penguin Books Australia Ltd, Ringwood, Victoria, Australia
Penguin Books Canada Ltd, 10 Alcorn Avenue, Toronto, Ontario, Canada M4V 3B2
Penguin Books (N.Z.) Ltd, 182–190 Wairau Road, Auckland 10, New Zealand
Penguin Books Ltd, Registered Offices: Harmondsworth, Middlesex, England

First published in 1992 by Viking, a division of Penguin Books USA Inc.

1 3 5 7 9 10 8 6 4 2

Copyright © Lisa Eisenberg, 1992
All rights reserved

LIBRARY OF CONGRESS CATALOGING-IN-PUBLICATION DATA
Eisenberg, Lisa. Lexie on her own / by Lisa Eisenberg. p. cm.
Summary: With Christmas around the corner and her world filled
with problems, Lexie must draw upon all her resources to
overcome some particularly harsh holiday blues.
ISBN 0-670-84489-6 : [1. Christmas—Fiction.
2. Family life—Fiction.] I. Title.
PZ7.E3458Lex 1992 [Fic]—dc20 91-40289 CIP AC

Printed in U.S.A.
Set in Times Roman

Without limiting the rights under copyright reserved above, no part of this
publication may be reproduced, stored in or introduced into a retrieval system, or
transmitted, in any form or by any means (electronic, mechanical, photocopying,
recording or otherwise), without the prior written permission of both the
copyright owner and the above publisher of this book.

For Kate, Annie, and Tommy,
who puzzle me every day

One

I am so lone-leeee . . . in the days since you left meeee . . . ''

The song crackled out over the skating rink's staticky speaker system. When Lexie Nielsen heard it, she sighed so gustily her breath made a huge frosty cloud around her head. How true, she thought. How true. She understood exactly what those corny old lyrics were talking about. She had never felt so lonely in her whole life.

She skated along the back fence, carefully focusing

her gaze straight down at the ice. She couldn't risk glancing up even for a few seconds. If she did, she might see the Figenbaums' house just across the street from the park. Then she would have to look at the big SOLD sign on the snow-covered front lawn. That, she knew, would be more than she could bear.

She came around the curve of the rink and saw two little boys in hockey uniforms charging straight for her.

"Watch it, bozo!" one of them shouted, punching the other boy in the arm.

"*You* watch it, stinkface!" the second one yelled back. He reached out to grab his friend around the neck and almost lost his balance. Both boys continued to race along at top speed, careening dangerously out of control as they went. Lexie threw herself sideways into the fence just in time to avoid being knocked down. She turned around to glare at the boys. As she did, she noticed a small crowd of people gathering in the center of the rink. She pushed off the fence and glided over in their direction.

"Isn't she terrific?" someone was saying.

"Unbelievable," another person agreed. "You know, I heard she's been taking lessons since she was two."

Lexie craned her neck to see whom the people were talking about. In the middle of the ice, she spotted a girl wearing a bulky blue sweater, a short, glittering skating skirt, and cream-colored tights. Even though the skater was twirling around in a breathtaking blur, Lexie had no trouble recognizing her. That mane of curly black hair could belong to one person only, and that was *the* Tara Lynch-Harrison.

"Hi, Lexie!" At the sound of her name, Lexie turned and saw her old friend, Cheryl Ingebrettson, skating clumsily toward her. As Lexie started to say hello, Cheryl tripped over the front tip of her own skate blade and staggered forward. Lexie caught her arm as she fell down on the ice.

She pulled Cheryl back up to a standing position and smiled. "You remind me of an old riddle, Cheryl," she said. "What's the hardest thing about learning to skate?"

Cheryl rolled her eyes and made a face. "I can't believe it, Lexie!" she exclaimed. "You're *still* going around telling riddles all the time? Even though we've been in fifth grade for over three months?"

Lexie quickly looked around, praying none of the other skaters had overheard Cheryl's insulting comment. Her already pink cheeks turned red with shame and dismay. What was going on here? Cheryl had always loved riddles before!

Lexie felt like knocking Cheryl back down onto the ice again but decided against it. These days, she couldn't afford to fight with one of her last remaining friends. She swallowed her pride, elbowed Cheryl in the ribs, and changed the subject. "Did you get a load of the outfit over there?" she asked, gesturing in Tara's direction. "I mean, is she showing off or what?"

She waited for Cheryl to laugh and agree with her, but instead her friend frowned in confusion. "What are you talking about, Lexie?"

"Duh, Cheryl. Tara Lynch-Harrison, of course. Where do you suppose she got that skirt? And don't you think she's probably freezing to death? It's ten below zero out here!"

Cheryl turned to gaze at Tara. "I think she looks beautiful," she breathed. "She looks just like a professional figure skater. They're supposed to dress like that."

"Maybe in the *Ice Capades* . . . ," Lexie began. She noticed Cheryl's rapt expression and swallowed her words. What was the point of going on? Cheryl wouldn't understand anyway. Come to think of it, Cheryl hadn't understood much of anything for a long time. Ever since she'd convinced her mother to let her get her ears pierced at the mall last summer, Cheryl had been a completely different person. It was almost as if her whole old personality had seeped out through two tiny holes in her earlobes.

Lexie shook her head and looked over at Tara again. "Well," she said, in an effort to be fair, "that *is* a pretty snowflake sweater she has on. I wonder where she gets all those blue sweaters she's always wearing. They look like they cost a million dollars each."

"They're to die for," Cheryl gushed. "Tara has the best clothes in the whole school! I can't figure out what in the world to wear to that holiday party she's having the day after Christmas. I mean, I heard she invited boys and everything! What are you wearing?"

This time even frozen cheeks couldn't mask the hot red flush that suddenly colored Lexie's face. Cheryl caught sight of her friend's expression and bit her lip. "You mean you didn't get an invitation?" she asked in dismay. "I'm sorry, Lexie. I heard she was inviting everybody!"

"Everybody who's anybody, I guess. And obviously that doesn't include me!" Lexie turned away from Cheryl and skated toward the warming house.

Cheryl sped after her. "I'm sorry, Lexie," she said again. "I didn't mean to hurt your feelings."

Lexie stopped so sharply her skate blades sprayed up a shower of ice flakes. She whirled around and put her hands on her hips. "You didn't hurt my feelings, Cheryl!" she said angrily. "What makes you think I care about stupid Tara Lynch-Harrison's stupid holiday party? I think she's a big, stupid show-off, and the last thing in the world I would want to do is go to her big, stupid party! And I think anyone who wants to go to her party is stupid."

Cheryl's big blue eyes opened wide, and she stared at Lexie without saying a word. For a few long seconds, Lexie glared back at her, her whole body throbbing with hot rage and wounded feelings.

"I'm sorry, Lexie," Cheryl finally said again. "I'm sorry I said anything about the party."

Cheryl's voice sounded small and quavery, and as she listened to it, Lexie's anger slowly began to cool. With a sudden rush of guilt, she remembered what a sweet friend Cheryl had always been and how much she hated upsetting anyone. "It's really okay, Cheryl," she said in a quieter voice. "Tara probably just invited a few special celebrities to her party. You should consider yourself lucky to be among the chosen."

Cheryl let out a long breath, and looked relieved. "Come on, Lex," she said with a smile. "Let's go buy a hot chocolate from the snack bar."

Lexie shook her head and sighed. "Nothing would make me happier. But, as usual, I'm broke."

"I'll treat you."

Lexie paused for a minute, the image of a mug of hot chocolate floating through her mind. Tiny puffs of steam wafted up from the warm cup. A glob of melting marshmallows swam on top of the rich brown pool.

It wasn't as if Cheryl didn't have the money, Lexie told herself, as her mouth began to water. Unlike her own stingy parents, Cheryl's mother and father handed out unlimited amounts of spending money *without* the

6

benefit of long, boring speeches on the value of a dollar. Cheryl would never even miss the pittance it would cost to buy an extra cup of hot chocolate.

"I'd love a hot . . . ," Lexie began. But as she spoke, she saw a blur of movement over Cheryl's shoulder. It was Tara Lynch-Harrison again. This time, instead of spinning, Tara was gliding, leaping, and twirling, all in one graceful, fluid motion. The people watching were applauding and shouting their approval.

A sour taste filled Lexie's mouth. Suddenly the thought of hot chocolate made her feel sick. "Thanks anyway," she told Cheryl. "But my mom wants me home early today." This was an out-and-out lie, but Lexie didn't care. All at once, she felt as if she had to get away from the skating rink *or else.*

"Okay," Cheryl said. "See you soon." She turned to rejoin the crowd around Tara, but then she turned back again. "By the way, Lex. You never told me. What *is* the hardest thing about learning to skate?"

"The ice," Lexie answered automatically. Cheryl rolled her eyes again, and Lexie grinned. The grin vanished the instant Cheryl was gone.

"What's the hardest thing about being in fifth grade?" Lexie asked herself out loud. "Having your best friend move to California. And having a coldhearted monster like Tara Lynch-Harrison move into town instead!"

Two

Lexie was still feeling sorry for herself fifteen minutes later as she walked up the Fiftieth Street hill toward home.

For one thing, the temperature was dropping steadily, and her nose, fingers, and toes were all painfully cold. But for another, in spite of what she'd said to Cheryl, she knew she really did care about not getting one of Tara's invitations. Even if the girl was a conceited show-off, it still hurt to be the only person in fifth grade who hadn't been invited to her party.

"Don't think about the stupid party anymore if it makes you feel so bad, you big dummy," she told herself under her breath. "Why don't you concentrate on something cheerful instead . . . like thinking up some riddles? Even if Cheryl the Sophisticated has outgrown them, it doesn't mean *you* have!"

Lexie had been making up riddles ever since she could remember. Even though a lot of them were corny, the mental game usually helped cheer her up when she was feeling bad. She looked around the street for a good riddle subject, but all she saw were piles of dirty snow.

"All right," she said, "snow it is. Let's see. What do you get if you cross a pile of snow with . . . something with sharp teeth like, say . . . a mad dog? Frostbite!" She snorted at her own joke, and her breath escaped in a frosty gust in front of her face.

"Okay," she continued. "That'll be my next subject. Cold. Cold cuts. Cold-blooded. Out in the cold. Cold shoulder. Cold heart . . . cold, cold, cold, *mean* heart, just like Tara Lynch-Harrison's! Why is Tara so stupid? Because the only thing she can keep in her head for five minutes *is* a cold!"

She snorted with laughter again, but then sighed when she realized her riddle game had brought her right back to the very subject she'd been trying to avoid. If only Debby were still here, she told herself. Then everything would be different. The two of them would have found a way of making a big joke out of Tara and

9

her invitations. They would have made each other laugh so hard the silly party wouldn't have seemed important at all.

But Debby isn't here, Lexie grimly reminded herself as she turned left onto Fremont Avenue. The Figenbaums had packed up their belongings and moved to California for good last August. Then, to make matters worse, Lexie's two other oldest friends had both mutated into new people over the summer. Cheryl Ingebrettson had turned into a clothes freak who talked on and on about boys and being popular. And Suzy Frankowski had been assigned to a different fifth grade class and was now hanging around with a whole new group of kids.

Even the new friends she'd made the year before were no longer around. Gretchen Dietz had moved into a bigger house in a fancier part of town. And Shirley Spitzer had started going to a special school for children with learning disabilities. One way or another, everyone had either changed or left altogether.

"Fifth grade really stinks," Lexie said out loud.

She trudged along the narrow path between the giant piled-up snowbanks on her street. Everyone on the block had dutifully cleared their walks after last night's big storm. Everyone but the Nielsens, that is. When she reached her own family's treacherous, ice-packed section of unshoveled sidewalk, Lexie winced. It had been her turn to do "snow squad" that morning. As usual, she'd conveniently forgotten all about it. She was sure she'd hear about it at dinner tonight.

She paused next to a towering snowbank and looked at the old dull-gray car parked by the curb. It belonged to her mother, and, because of its habit of breaking down in the middle of traffic, her father had nicknamed it "Bea Ware."

The car was rusty and battered and made an alarming grinding sound when it drove. Usually Lexie was embarrassed by the sight of it. But today, she leaned over and gave the car a sympathetic pat. "You look like I feel, Bea. Alone and forgotten."

She turned away from the car and climbed the icy front steps, clinging to the frosty iron railing as she went. Inside the house, it was as quiet as a graveyard. "Mom?" Lexie called.

There was no answer. Lexie hadn't really expected one. If Mrs. Nielsen was home she was probably down in the basement, hunched over the computer, mumbling to herself. She'd been slaving over her master's degree thesis for several long, hard months now. It was called "Developing Coping Skills for Handling Stress in Family Life," and she was completely absorbed in it.

Too absorbed in it, Lexie thought. Mrs. Nielsen had become so involved in her work, it was almost as if the thesis had taken control of her, just the way It had taken control of Charles Wallace in *A Wrinkle in Time*. After several frustrating tries at communicating with the glassy-eyed creature in the basement, Lexie's coping skills had been stressed to their maximum limit. After that, she'd decided to try handling her life without a mother until the thesis was finished.

She dropped her skates on the living room floor and kicked off her frozen boots. Then she opened the little glass door of the mail chute set into the wall in the front hall. She was hoping to find a long-overdue letter from Debby in California, but she was disappointed. As usual, the mail chute was empty.

In her gray cotton socks, she padded into the kitchen, where she helped herself to a huge handful of pretzels from the open bag on the counter. Then she went to look for Fido, the Figenbaums' former cat, who was now living with the Nielsens. She found him sprawled in his favorite place—on the mat by the basement door. It was the sunniest spot in the house.

"Hi, you fuzzy old fat cat," she told him. "Did you miss me?" She knelt down and nuzzled one of the cat's battered gray ears. Even though he was only three years old, Fido had already been in hundreds of vicious cat fights. His nose and the top of his head were ridged with battle scars.

Lexie scratched under his chin, and Fido opened one yellow eye and blinked at her. She hauled him up from the floor and draped him over one arm. Leaving behind a salty trail of pretzel crumbs, she headed up to her room.

In the upstairs hall, she hurried right past her sixteen-year-old brother Daniel's room but slowed down by her oldest sister Karen's. Technically, of course, the room now belonged to her other sister Faith, who had moved into it when Karen left for college in September. But Lexie just couldn't get used to that idea.

Even though Karen had been gone for three months, her presence still seemed to hover in her sacred room, ordering her little sisters to keep their hands off her precious stuff. To Lexie's intense surprise, she'd caught herself starting to miss Karen lately. In fact, though she hadn't admitted it to anyone, she could hardly wait for Karen to come home for Winter Break on Sunday.

Lexie cocked her head and stopped chewing pretzels for a few seconds. Had she heard a noise coming out of Karen's room? Yes! She could definitely hear the crinkle of paper being folded. She pushed open the door and walked in.

"Lexie! Do you have slush for brains? How many times do I have to tell you to knock before you come into my room? Can't you see I'm wrapping Christmas presents in here?" Faith picked up a little gray catnip mouse and carefully placed it on a square of green and gold paper. "Turn Fido's face away," she commanded. "I don't want him to see what I got him."

Lexie laughed. "Oh, he's just a sleepy old thing," she said. "He won't know the difference."

"Well, at least you could stop holding him over your

arm like that. You're squashing his fat stomach, and he looks like he's going to throw up."

"His stomach wouldn't be so fat if you'd stop sneaking him up here and feeding him Kitty Yum-Yums all the time!" Lexie peered around Faith's shoulder at the pile of boxes on the bed. "I hope you got me something good this year. How come you're wrapping your presents so early? Christmas isn't for two weeks! I don't have anything for anybody yet."

"Well, when *are* you planning to buy your presents, Little Miss Lazy? At the last minute as usual?" Faith gazed at her sister with narrowed, all-knowing eyes. "And what are you planning to use for money, anyway? I happen to know you've borrowed ahead on your allowance for the next six months. And I also happen to know what you spent it on . . . *Mad Magazines* and Cheez Doodles!"

"You 'happen' to know an awful lot about my business, don't you, you nosy creep!" Lexie shouted. "If you weren't always snooping around corners pretending to do your homework while you're listening in on Mom and Daddy's conversations, maybe then you'd—"

"Get out of here, Lexie!" Faith interrupted. "This is my room, and I order you to get out!"

"It's not your room for long, sweetheart," Lexie said nastily. "Remember, Karen's coming home from college Sunday."

Faith's eyes glittered. "I'm not leaving," she muttered darkly. "They'll have to drag me out of here."

"I'd be glad to help them. It sounds like fun."

"*Get out!* And stop squashing that poor cat's stomach. He doesn't just belong to *you,* you know! He's the whole family's pet!"

Lexie stuck out her tongue and left. "What does she know, anyway?" she asked Fido as she stomped into her own room. "You don't care how I hold you, do you?"

She put Fido down on her unmade bed next to a pile of stuffed bears, dogs, tigers, and seals. The cat flipped over onto his back and immediately fell asleep. Whenever Lexie's father saw him lying in that position, he said it looked as if Fido were playing "dead dog." The dead dog position was the reason the Nielsens had changed the cat's name from "Tabby" to "Fido" when they'd inherited him from the Figenbaums.

Lexie smiled at the sight of Fido's four white paws sticking straight up in the air. She opened the top drawer of her dresser and rummaged around until she found the little pink camera her grandmother had sent her for her last birthday. Then she started snapping pictures of the sleeping cat.

"I want to be sure and get a close-up of your big fat stomach, Fido," she said. "It's really your best feature." She used up the roll of film and put the camera on her night table.

"I remembered a riddle you'd really like today," she

told the cat. "If there are ten cats on a boat and one jumps off, how many cats do you have left?" She crawled onto the bed and curled up next to Fido. "You probably think the answer is nine, right? But it's not. The answer is: there are *no* cats left on the boat. Why not? Because they were all copycats!"

She reached over and stroked Fido's lumpy forehead and warm, soft body. "That was a good one, wasn't it? I'm so glad you appreciate my humor. You're about the only one who does around here anymore. Wait till you hear what happened to me today."

She poured the entire story of Cheryl and the ice skating rink and Tara's party into the cat's gently twitching ear. "Can you believe it, Fido?" she said when she'd finished. "Cheryl thought Tara was inviting everybody, but I hadn't even heard about the stupid party! And to top things off, stupid Faith just reminded me I don't have any Christmas presents for anybody yet. And my bank account is negative zero. And *please* don't suggest I make things for people. You know I can't sew or do pottery or draw or anything. So where am I supposed to come up with five Christmas presents?"

She rose up on her elbow and stared at the cat until he opened his eyes.

"What's that you say, Fido?" she went on. "You think I should beg for more money from my parents and promise to pay it back after Christmas?"

She flopped back down on the pillow and sighed. "I

guess you're right. I mean, it would be pretty mortifying not to have anything to give anybody on Christmas morning. So I suppose, as you point out, my only choice is to *make* Mom and Daddy give me some money."

She looked over at Fido, and smiled. "Thanks for the suggestion, you fuzzy old cat," she whispered. "It's nice to know at least *somebody* around here still cares about me!"

Three

Dinner that night was broiled haddock, which Lexie detested. Normally, she would have loudly complained about being forced to eat fish, which everyone knew she hated, but tonight she sat quietly at her place. When no one was watching, she slipped little pieces of fish under the table to Fido, who was eagerly waiting under her chair. Meanwhile, she plotted and replotted the best plan of attack for convincing her father to give her another advance on her allowance.

"Terrific haddock, Daddy," she said when all her fish was gone. "Mmmm."

Faith shot her a suspicious look, but Mr. Nielsen beamed. "Well, thank you, Lexie," he said. "You know, the trick is all in the seasonings. Tonight I tried a dusting of paprika combined with tarragon, and, if I do say so myself, the results were quite successful. Don't you think it was delicious, Barbara?"

Mrs. Nielsen didn't answer him, and everyone turned to look at her. She was staring down at her plate as if she'd never seen a plate before. She hadn't eaten a single bite of her fish. "Delicious," she repeated mechanically. "Delicious."

Mr. Nielsen sighed and closed his eyes. His lips didn't move, but Lexie and Faith knew he was counting to ten inside his head. Though Mr. Nielsen was very careful not to say anything out loud, the whole family knew he'd begun to resent Mrs. Nielsen's thesis as much as they all did.

"The haddock *was* delicious, Daddy," Lexie said quickly. "Best meal I ever had. A truly scrumptious piece of fish."

Her father opened his eyes again and gazed at her. Lexie thought she might have overdone it, but there was no going back now. "The fish was so delicious," she went on, "it reminded me of all the delicious Christmas dinners we've had here at this very table. And that

19

made me wonder if it might be possible to get another small advance on my allowance. You know, just so I could buy everybody some really nice presents this year?"

Faith snorted so loudly the sound waves rattled the glasses on the table. Mr. Nielsen frowned and shook his head. "Lexie, we've been over and over this with you. You simply cannot have any more money until you acquire some decent spending habits!"

"But how can I acquire decent spending habits when I don't have any money to practice with?" Lexie whined.

"Well, when you start accumulating an allowance again in . . . what is it . . . three months?"

"Six," Faith said promptly. "She doesn't get any allowance for six months."

"Six months," Mr. Nielsen continued, "then you can begin practicing how to budget your money more wisely."

"But what about Christmas? How am I supposed to give anybody anything for Christmas?"

"You know we've never encouraged you children to give expensive presents, Lexie," her father said. "I'm sure we'd all appreciate something homemade. Say a drawing from school or perhaps a poem you've written . . . Faith, are you all right? Are you gagging on a fishbone?"

Lexie glowered at her sister, and Faith stopped pretending to choke.

"How about trying to earn some money, Lexie?" she said. "You know, like everybody else in the family? Karen works in the library at college, Daniel is serving fries at McDonald's even as we speak, and I baby-sit every single Saturday!"

"Well, aren't you just the most perfect thing in the world?" Lexie began. "Maybe you'd like us all to start calling you 'Your Royal Perfectness' or 'Your Gracious Goodness' or—"

"Girls!" Mr. Nielsen broke in sharply. He looked down at the other end of the table for support, but Mrs. Nielsen was still gazing at her plate. "Please stop your bickering! Lexie, you may not have an advance on your allowance. And, Faith, mind your own business."

He clasped his hands together and smiled at them. "And now, on to a more pleasant subject. I know it's hard to believe, but it's already time for the Audubon Society's annual winter bird count! Who's coming with me this year?"

Faith and Lexie stared at each other, suddenly united in their dismay. The winter bird count was something to avoid at any cost. "I can't go!" Faith said hastily. "I'm baby-sitting Saturday. And besides, I have a ton of homework."

"I can't go either," Lexie said desperately. "I'm . . . I'm . . . uh . . . "

"I think you should go with Daddy, honey. You've been moping around here so much since Debby moved.

It would do you good to get out of the house for a change."

At the unexpected sound of Mrs. Nielsen's voice, everyone turned to gawk at her. She blinked at them. "Why are you all looking at me like that?" she asked. "Did I say something so extraordinary?"

"No, Mom," Faith said. "Actually, you said something *ordinary*. And *that*'s why we're all looking at you!"

Mrs. Nielsen raised her eyebrows. "Really? What *can* you be talking about?"

"Well," Faith said uncertainly, "it's just that . . . well, you have to admit you've been a little . . . well . . . *distracted* lately, Mom."

"We've been thinking of calling Rent-A-Parent for a replacement for you, Mom!" Lexie said. "You've been acting like a real zombie."

"Oh, *have* I? Have I *really?*" Mrs. Nielsen leaned forward in her chair and glared at all of them. When she spoke, her voice was low and intense. "Do you want to know what I think? I think all of you might be just a little more understanding about the kind of pressure I'm operating under. Do you have any idea what my stress level must be? Do you comprehend that every single solitary word in this thesis has to be *absolutely perfect?* Do you? *Do* you?"

A long silence followed Mrs. Nielsen's speech. Finally, Mr. Nielsen cleared his throat. "Ah . . . yes," he said. "Yes indeed, I think we do comprehend that,

Barbara. And I think we also all agree with you [when?] you say that Lexie needs to get out of the hous[e and] be with other people more." He turned to [Lexie]. "Maybe you could invite a friend to come along [on the] bird count. What about one of those other girl[s who] always used to come over here? What were [their] names?"

"Cheryl and Suzy," Lexie said dully.

"Right!" Mr. Nielsen nodded enthusiastically. [And] what about that new girl you told us about at the [be]inning of the school year? Perhaps she'd enjoy g[oing.] After all, being new to town, she might not have [had] a chance to make many friends yet, and—"

"New girl?" Lexie interrupted.

"Yes, I distinctly recall your mentioning a new [girl] who joined your class in September. You said s[he] moved here from Chicago, I believe."

"You're talking about Tara Lynch-Harrison!" L[exie] was incredulous. "You're actually saying you w[ant] me to ask Tara Lynch-Harrison to come on the fr[eez]ing, boring, nightmare, disgusting winter bird co[unt] with us?"

"Lexie doesn't like Tara Lynch-Harrison, Dadd[y,"] Faith said. "She's jealous of her."

Lexie jumped up so suddenly her chair toppled o[ver] backward and crashed to the floor. "Just shut up a[nd] butt out of my life, Faith!" she shrieked. "I am n[ot] jealous of that conceited show-off, Tara Lync[h-]

23

Harrison! I just can't stand her. And I can't stand *you,* either!"

She bent over and scooped up Fido, who'd narrowly missed being hit by the falling chair. Clutching the cat in both arms, she tore out the door and escaped up the stairs to the safety of her own room.

Four

Two hours later, Lexie and Fido crept downstairs and went into the kitchen to make cookies. The house was so still that after a while Lexie began to wonder where everyone could be. Daniel, she decided, must still be at work. Her father was probably in his bedroom listening to Mozart and sorting old bird photographs. Faith was undoubtedly closeted away upstairs doing her homework again and again until it was perfect. And her mother . . .

Lexie crossed the kitchen to the basement door and

listened hard. Sure enough, she heard the gentle clacking sound of Mrs. Nielsen's fingers tapping away at the computer keyboard. Poor Mom, Lexie thought. It was hard to imagine having to work that hard on *anything*.

She was busily stirring a bag of chocolate chips into the cookie batter when Daniel hobbled into the kitchen, home from his job at McDonald's.

"Who the heck was supposed to do snow squad this morning, anyway?" he scowled. "The front walk is like a bobsled run! I just fell halfway down the steps and twisted my ankle!"

Lexie clucked her tongue in sympathy, but wisely decided not to say anything about the snow squad. "That reminds me of a riddle," she said instead.

"What doesn't?"

"What kind of disease *helps* you be better in sports?"

"I don't know, Lex. But I'm sure you're going to tell me."

"Athlete's foot!"

Daniel groaned and made a face. "That was definitely not one of your best efforts, Lexie."

Lexie nodded. "I know. I can't help it. I'm off my form these days."

Daniel limped over to the counter and peered into the mixing bowl. "Hot dog!" he said. "Chocolate chippers. Let me have the beater."

"Help yourself," Lexie told him. "But you'd better not let Mom see you. She'll give you that speech about the dangers of eating raw eggs and getting salmonella poisoning."

Daniel laughed. "You've got to be kidding." He licked a big glob of batter from the beater. "These days Mom wouldn't notice if I ate a whole raw pig!"

Lexie giggled. "You should have seen her at dinner tonight. She had one sane moment, and we all thought she might be turning normal again. But then she went into this tirade about her stress level. It was scary."

"The Mom Who Came from Outer Space," Daniel said. He finished with the beater and tried to take a fingerful of batter from the bowl.

Lexie pushed him away. "Knock it off!" she yelled. "This is my dinner. You can lick the bowl when I'm finished."

"I'll wait." Daniel picked up the cat and sat down at the kitchen table. Then he started scratching Fido's round white stomach. The cat growled and savagely dug his claws into Daniel's hand.

"Yowch!"

"Stop scratching his stomach like that!" Lexie ordered. "You know he hates that!"

"Geez, that hurts!" With a pained expression, Daniel pried the cat's needlelike claws out of his skin. When his hand was free, he used it to scratch behind Fido's ears. Instantly, a loud purring filled the kitchen.

"Daniel," Lexie said as she spooned mounds of cookie batter onto a tray, "do you happen to have any extra money lying around that you might be willing to let me borrow?"

"Sure I do, Lex. I'd be glad to lend you a couple thou. But unfortunately, all my funds are tied up in the stock market at the moment."

Lexie glowered at him. "It's not funny!" she said, yanking open the oven door and sliding in the cookie tray. "It's almost Christmas, and I'm completely broke. And I don't have a single present for anybody!"

"Can't you do some work or something?"

Lexie slammed the oven door. "In case you haven't noticed, Daniel, the job market for ten-year-olds is pretty tight these days!"

Daniel got to his feet, dumping an indignant Fido onto the floor. "Well, you don't have to buy me a present, anyway," he said. "Just mix me up a big vat of cookie dough." Before Lexie could stop him, he reached over and dug out a big fingerful of batter from the mixing bowl.

He headed out of the kitchen, but turned around before he got to the door. "By the way, Lex, have you been taking my *Sports Illustrated*s lately? I haven't gotten one for two weeks!"

"Oh, right, Daniel. If I want to see a bunch of smelly athletes, I don't need to look in a magazine. All I have to do is come watch you and your sweaty friends playing soccer!"

Daniel shook his fist at her, but he was smiling. "Call

me when the cookies are ready," he said. He left t
kitchen and went up the stairs to his room.

Lexie looked down at Fido and shrugged. "He v
a lot of help, wasn't he, cat?" Fido lay down and flipp
over onto his back. "My thoughts exactly," Lexie t
him. "My brother is a self-centered moron." Even
she said the words, Lexie knew they weren't true. Wh
Daniel might be self-centered sometimes, he was
opposite of a moron. The high point of Mr. and N
Nielsen's lives had always been going to parent-teac
conferences about Daniel. Mr. Nielsen claimed
teachers inevitably grew misty-eyed and tried to l
him when they found out whose father he was.

Lexie's parent-teacher conferences, on the ot
hand, were an entirely different affair. At Lexie's c
ferences, according to her parents, the teachers got
her messy papers, sadly shook their heads, and lectu
about wasted potential. "Perhaps it has to do with
birth order," Lexie had once overheard her mot
telling a friend on the phone. "But Lexie is simply
a goal-oriented child. She just doesn't focus in on pi
lems the way Daniel did at that age."

"Mr. Super-Achiever Daniel," Lexie muttered
Fido. She opened the oven and carefully took out
hot tray of cookies. "What problems does he hav
focus in on, anyway? Nothing worse than a few
issues of *Sports Illustrated*! He makes millions of do
at McDonald's. And he has millions of friends,

29

I wonder how he'd feel if all his jock pals suddenly moved out of town!" She reached for the spatula and lifted the cookies off the tray. She put six onto a small plastic plate, and the rest onto a flattened-out brown grocery bag.

"Come on, Fido," she said, reaching down for the cat. "Let's go upstairs and write a letter to Debby. I know it's her turn to write me, but who cares? She's the only friend I have left in the world! Except for you, that is."

She picked up the plate of cookies and carried it and Fido up the stairs to her room. There, she cleared a space in the middled of her cluttered bed, and curled up with her math notebook. On the last page she wrote:

Dear Debby,

Greetings from Fido (formerly Tabby) and me! Please excuse any crumbs I get on this, but we just baked cookies. Your ex-cat was a big help, as usual.

Remember that new girl, Tara, I wrote you about who everybody thinks is such hot stuff? Well, now it seems she's having a holiday party, and she invited everybody but me! Can you believe it? Do you think it might be my breath? I saw her down at the skating rink today, and she was dressed up just like your old *Ice Capades* Barbie doll! The only thing she didn't have was those little purple plastic high-heeled skates! Cheryl was there, too, drooling all over the ice and telling me

how fantastic Tara was. You wouldn't believe how much she's changed since last year.

How are things going in California? You must be pretty busy since you never bothered to answer my last letter.(!!!!!) Please write soon.

I am your best friend

till butter flies,

Lexie

P.S. Here is my father's latest terrible riddle.

Question: Why did gloomy Lexie have to buy such big clothes?

Answer: Because she was a person of great sighs!

Five

Lexie had a lot of trouble sleeping that night. Her problems began when she tried to keep Fido in the bed with her. As usual, it didn't work. The instant the lights went out, the cat's sleepy yellow eyes popped open, and he was transformed into a restless, prowling Creature of the Darkness. Every time Lexie picked him up and tucked him in, he fought his way out from under the blankets, leaped off the bed, and raked his claws on the closed door.

Finally she gave up and let him leave the room. In

an instant, he pelted down the stairs and yowled to be let out into the backyard. A few seconds later, Lexie heard her father speaking to the cat. "Are you serious about this, Fido old boy? It's freezing outside! Wouldn't you rather stay inside with the folks?"

Fido's answer was a long, indignant, *"Miaaaaa-ooooouuu!"*

"All right, old boy! You've made your intentions abundantly clear." The front door creaked open. "Be on your way. But don't stay out too late! Don't get into any fights! And *don't* catch any birds!"

After that, Lexie tried to settle down to sleep alone. But just as she drifted off, the deep boom of her father's voice rumbled up the steps again. This time, it was answered by the higher murmur of her mother's voice. From the direction of the sounds, Lexie could tell that her parents were settling down at the dining room table. Her body tensed. Uh-oh, she thought. Her mother and father were about to have one of their monthly bill-paying sessions.

She was right. Within a few minutes, the voices grew louder, and Lexie could understand the words.

"Who charged this skirt at Dayton's?" her father was asking. "And why did it cost so much?"

"That was for Faith," her mother answered. "She really needed something new for school."

"But she has a whole closetful of clothes up there!"

"I know, I know." Mrs. Nielsen's voice grew quieter

as she explained about the skirt, and her words became a gentle murmur again.

Lexie clenched her teeth. Suddenly, she yearned for brooding, moody Faith to be back in the room with her, curled up in her old bed in the opposite corner. Even though the girls had never talked out loud about the bill-paying sessions, the two of them had an unspoken agreement about them. They passionately hated the bill-paying sessions. But somehow, listening in on them had been easier with Faith right there in the room.

"Frank, did you really need a new tripod for your camera? What was wrong with the old one?"

Now it was Mr. Nielsen's turn to rumble an explanation. Lexie shut her eyes tight and imagined the scene taking place downstairs. The dining room table would be covered with envelopes and different-colored bills from stores, mechanics, utilities, doctors, dentists, magazines, and charitable organizations. Her parents would be sorting the bills into two piles. One pile would be for bills that had to be paid right away. The other would be for bills that could be put off for another month.

"Look at this phone bill! We simply must explain to Karen that calling collect is much more expensive than regular calling. And has the dentist raised his rates all of a sudden? There's only one checkup listed here. Why's the bill so much?"

"Lexie had a cavity," her mother explained. "She needed a filling."

"Well, what did he fill it with? Gold? Diamonds? Platinum?"

"I don't know, Frank, but I think we'd better pay it now. The date on it is several months old. In fact, most of these bills seem to be old ones. Heaven only knows what we'll do when the new ones come in!"

Lexie cringed under her blankets and wondered if she could have saved the family some money if she'd done a better job of brushing her teeth. Guiltily, she remembered all those nights she'd been too lazy to brush them at all and had gone to bed with nasty food particles still left in her mouth. While she'd slept, those tiny pieces of bread, potatoes, Cheez Doodles, peanut butter, and haddock had been hard at work creating the cavity that was about to put her family into the poorhouse.

She flopped over onto her stomach and pulled her blanket up over her head in an effort to muffle the sound of her parents' voices. Just then, she heard angry footsteps stomping along the hallway outside her room. They stopped at the top of the stairs.

"Hey! Could you *please* keep it quiet down there? Some of us are trying to sleep!"

Lexie could almost feel the sudden shocked silence rising up the stairs from the dining room. For once, she felt grateful for Faith's horrible temper and sharp tongue. She'd always been pretty sure her mother and father hadn't known the kids could hear the bill-paying sessions, and it was high time someone told them about it. Still, if that someone were going to get in trouble for shouting at her parents, Lexie would rather have it be Faith than her!

Her sister's footsteps clomped back along the hallway. Lexie strained to hear more conversation from downstairs, but everything remained quiet. Her parents must have terminated the bill-paying session, or else they were whispering so softly Lexie couldn't hear them. Either way, the silence was wonderful. With a sigh of relief, Lexie turned over onto her side, clutched the edge of her blanket, and finally managed to fall asleep.

Six

Tara Lynch-Harrison was the first person Lexie saw at school the next day. Though Lexie usually dawdled over her breakfast and put off leaving home until the last possible second, that morning she'd gulped down a piece of toast and hurried out the door as early as she could. After she'd finished her letter to Debby the night before, she'd discovered three forgotten, long-overdue homework assignments wedged inside the back of her math notebook. She was hoping to polish them off before the other kids arrived for the day.

But she didn't get any time to work. When she started to sit down at her desk, she found a note taped to her chair. It said: *Lex: Have to talk to you about something urgently* important! *SOON!—Cheryl.*

Lexie looked at the note and frowned. Why hadn't Cheryl called her if she had something "urgently important" to tell her? she wondered. Then she remembered. Cheryl's parents had taken her phone privileges away because she'd been spending so much time calling up her friends. Mr. and Mrs. Ingebrettson had forbidden their daughter to so much as touch the phone for two whole weeks.

The punishment had to be driving her friend crazy, Lexie thought with a smile. These days Cheryl *lived* to talk on the phone! She stuffed the note into her back pocket and decided not to worry about it. Cheryl's message probably wasn't "urgently important" anyway. To her, "urgently important" meant the label had fallen off the back pocket of her designer jeans.

Lexie sat down at her desk and took out her math papers. Just then, Tara walked into the classroom. As usual, she was wearing one of the many beautiful, hand-knit blue sweaters that exactly matched the color of her eyes. But for once she wasn't surrounded by a group of fawning friends.

When Tara came in, Lexie flushed and ducked her head. She hunched forward over her homework, and tried to act as if she were completely absorbed in finding the lowest common denominator between two fractions. To her astonishment, out of the corner of her eye, she saw Tara strolling over toward her desk.

"Hi, Lexie," she said cheerfully. "Aren't those problems murder? I haven't turned mine in yet, either."

Lexie sat up straight and stared at the other girl. Though she struggled to control her face, she could feel her mouth forming into a slack-jawed, idiotic gape. How can Tara be doing this? she dumbly asked herself. How can she be acting like she hasn't done anything to me?

Frantically she tried to think of something devastatingly cutting to say. "Uh . . . ," she began. "Mmmmmbungah . . . "

Tara chattered on as if Lexie hadn't spoken. "Somebody told me you really like riddles," she said. "Have you heard the one about the math book? It goes: Why are you lucky if your dog eats your math book?"

"Uh . . . uh . . . "

"Because then you don't have any more problems!" Tara flashed her perfect white smile. "Isn't that a scream? I just wish it could be that easy to get rid of math problems! Don't you?"   ·

Lexie was saved from having to say "uh" again by the arrival of Mr. Lange, their large, bushy-haired fifth grade teacher.

"Let's save the gab sessions for later, kidlets," he said, slapping his huge, hammy hands together. "The sooner you grab your seats, the sooner we can rock and roll."

Gab sessions! Lexie repeated to herself as Tara walked away. Gab sessions were supposed to be between *two* people. Her conversation with Tara had sounded more like an interview between a person and an ape!

She bent down over her math homework again, her face still hot with embarrassment. She wrote her name at the top of the paper and then angrily scratched a series of dark lines through the L. What had come over her? she wondered. Why had she mumbled like that? What hadn't she said something clever, like "I don't have any problems with *math,* Tara. But I do have a few problems with *you!*" or, "Would you mind moving away from my desk, Tara? Your big, fat sweater is blocking the light!" or, "Maybe you would have had a chance to do your math homework, Tara, if you hadn't wasted so much time writing all those party invitations!"

But had she made any of those witty remarks? Nooo! All Lexie had been able to say was "uh" and "mmbungah!" Tara must think she was a complete dunce!

Desperately, she reminded herself that she didn't care what Tara thought of her—that, in fact, she already knew what Tara thought of her. Tara didn't like her. She'd proven that by leaving Lexie out of her precious holiday party.

But then why had Tara acted so nice just now? Lexie glanced across the room and saw Tara whispering and giggling with Cheryl, who sat right next to her. Suddenly, Lexie felt sure she understood exactly why Tara had been so friendly. Tara liked to have an audience, and Lexie had been the only other person in the room! If one single solitary other soul had been around, Tara would have ignored Lexie, just the way she always did.

Elementary, my dear Watson, Lexie thought. She wished Debby were there so she could share her brilliant deduction with someone. She sighed, put her elbows on her desk, propped up her chin on her hands, and allowed herself to reminisce about last Christmas. Because the Figenbaums were Jewish, Debby had always joked that Lexie owed her eight presents every December, one for each day of Hanukkah. Last year, Lexie had baked her a different-sized chocolate chip cookie for each day of the holiday, starting with a penny-sized cookie the first day and ending with a Frisbee-sized cookie the eighth.

Debby had saved all of the cookies until the last day of Hanukkah. Then the two of them had carved an igloo out of a snowbank on Lexie's street and crawled inside for a big cookie pig out. After that, Debby had given Lexie her Christmas present. It had been a riddle encyclopedia in which you could look up a riddle to fit almost any subject you could imagine. Lexie had read it from cover to cover.

"The Big Dipper is not officially a constellation." Mr. Lange's voice woke Lexie from her daydream. "It's really a part of the constellation Ursa Major, the Big Bear. The Big Dipper is called an asterism."

Though Lexie usually enjoyed Mr. Lange's astronomy lessons, today she just couldn't seem to get interested. As she gazed up at the rainbow pattern on the back of the teacher's oversized tie-dyed T-shirt, she fought the urge to put her head down on her desk and close her eyes. She could hear people whispering on the other side of the room and felt sure they had to be Tara and Cheryl.

She forced herself to think about something else. With her thumbnail, she stabbed a deep half-circle in the side of her eraser. After several more jabs, the series of little curved gouges started to form a picture on the dirty pink surface. The picture looked exactly like a dollar sign. *Aha!* Lexie thought. She'd found the perfect way to spend the morning. She'd daydream up a way of earning money to buy Christmas presents.

"At about forty degrees north latitude," Mr. Lange said, "the following constellations are considered North Circumpolar Constellations. That's because they look like they're circling the polestar, Polaris, and they don't set."

Money, Lexie thought. With unseeing eyes, she stared at the pattern of stars the teacher was drawing on the board. Money, money, money. Sometimes it seemed as if her parents never really thought about anything else. She frowned as she remembered last night's bill-paying session and her father's serious face as he lectured her about her own poor spending habits. She hadn't liked hearing it, but she knew he was right. Though she was always telling herself not to spend it, the little money she had always seemed to slip through her fingers like melted butter.

Of course, Lexie thought, the main problem was that she never had enough money to begin with. Most of the other kids she knew, like Cheryl and Suzy and even Debby before she'd moved, spent a lot more than she did. They bought all the *Mad Magazine*s and Cheez Doodles they wanted. When they ran out of money, their parents gave them more! It was as simple as that.

But Lexie's parents always had to be different about everything. Lately, they'd been *really* different, particularly her mother. Lexie frowned as she thought about Mrs. Nielsen, lost in a fog at the end of the dinner table, quietly obsessing about Coping Skills. The previous night's family conversation replayed itself in Lexie's mind, and the beginnings of an idea nagged at the edge of her consciousness.

She knew it had something to do with a comment she'd made to her mother, and something to do with a way of making money. Frantically, she tried to recapture the thought. But it was no use. As suddenly as it had appeared, the idea was gone, shut up in some far-off storage locker in the back of her brain.

"So much for the stars!" Mr. Lange bellowed from the front of the room. "What say we put in a little reading time here?"

The class cheered and burst into applause. All the kids loved listening to Mr. Lange read. He used a lot of funny voices and sound effects, and sometimes went so far as to act out a scene from a book as if he were putting on a play. Lexie stopped gouging her eraser and looked up expectantly. Mr. Lange had finished reading *The Phantom Tollbooth* to the class the day before. That meant that today he would be starting in on a new book.

"I thought we'd crack open *The Witches,* by Roald Dahl," the teacher told the class.

Most of the kids clapped again, but Lexie felt a twinge of disappointment. It wasn't that she didn't like *The Witches.* She loved it. In fact, she loved it so much she'd read it at least six times. She'd been hoping Mr. Lange would be performing a book she'd never heard of before.

The teacher began reading in a creepy, ominous voice. As the familiar description of traditional witches washed over Lexie, she decided she wouldn't mind hearing the story one more time. She settled down to listen, picking up her pencil to doodle on a blank page of her social studies notebook. Slowly, without Lexie's really planning it, the doodle began to take shape. First, a pointed black hat emerged. Then a long black cape and a crooked broomstick.

Soon the witch looked so deliciously mean and hag-like that Lexie forgot all about listening to Mr. Lange and threw herself into her drawing instead. A little smile played across her lips as she penciled in a thick mop of black curly hair, an oversized toothy smile, and a pair of huge, round eyes. She even got out her markers so she could color the collar of a blue sweater peeping out from under the witch's black cape.

The witch was a hideous masterpiece. Lexie fiddled with it off and on for the rest of the day. Whenever Mr. Lange wasn't looking, she pulled out the drawing and added another detail. She even stayed in at recess to work on it, pretending not to notice Cheryl, who was standing by the doorway, waving and motioning to get her attention.

Five minutes before the final bell of the day, she put on the last two flourishes. The first was a pair of ridiculously large ice skates stuck onto the bottom of the witch's scrawny legs. The second was a speech bubble coming out of the witch's mouth. Inside the bubble, it said, "Cackle, cackle, cackle. How do you spell *conceited?* T-A-R-A!"

The bell jangled, and everyone scrambled to clean off their desks and load up their backpacks. "Let's hustle, gang!" said Mr. Lange. He smacked his big hands together again, and began herding the class out into the hall. Lexie didn't even notice. She remained at her desk, gazing with satisfaction at her repulsive witch.

All at once, she noticed how quiet the room was. The only sound she could hear was Mr. Lange's voice coming in from the hallway, screaming at everybody to have a nice weekend or else.

Lexie grabbed up her books and hurled them into her backpack. She started to stuff her drawing into one of her notebooks, but then she paused. She stared at the picture so hard it began to look real. She could almost hear it bewitching her. "Do it," it seemed to whisper. "Go on and do it."

Suddenly, Lexie darted across the room. She raised the top of Tara's desk and thrust the drawing inside. She had to move quickly so she wouldn't get caught. But she still took the time to make sure the witch was lying face-up. That way Tara would be certain to see it first thing Monday morning.

Seven

Thick, soft snow started falling on the way home from school. In spite of herself, Lexie felt her heavy spirits begin to lighten. The big, fat, sticky flakes were her favorite kind. They were the perfect building material for igloos, forts, and snowpeople. Maybe, Lexie thought hopefully, Faith wouldn't be in an overly mature mood this afternoon. It just might be possible to coax her outside for a snowball fight.

She opened her mouth and let a huge clump of flakes land on her tongue. As she did, she suddenly remembered the idea that had flitted through her mind in school. She snapped her mouth shut and narrowed her eyes in thought. In an instant, she recognized that the idea was a good one. It was the best money-making plan she'd ever come up with. There was just one thing wrong with it. In order to make the plan succeed, Lexie was actually going to have to do some work!

In spite of that, she was excited and eager to tell someone about her brainstorm. She hurried the rest of the way home and raced up the steep, treacherously icy steps to her house.

"Mom!" she yelled as she burst through the front door. "Faith! Daniel!"

There was no answer, of course. Somehow, the house seemed even quieter than ever. "For Pete's sake!" Lexie said out loud. "Am I the only person who lives here anymore?"

She dumped her snowy backpack and boots on the middle of the living room rug and stomped through the house to the kitchen. "Yo, Fido!" she called. "Come here and let me tell you about my great plan!"

The cat didn't respond, and Lexie went to his favorite spot to search for him. But the mat by the basement door was empty. Lexie made a face. Faith probably had poor Fido trapped upstairs in her room, she thought. Stuffing him with Kitty Yum-Yums so he'd be even fatter than he already was.

She went back into the kitchen and started rummaging through the cupboard, searching for a decent snack. She'd just discovered half a bag of chocolate chips when her sister walked into the room.

"Say, Faith," Lexie said. "Do you think it's safe to eat these? The chips are all kind of white and crumbly-looking. Just how ancient do you suppose they are?"

Faith stared at her. "Lexie . . . "

"Oh, well," Lexie went on. She popped a handful of chips into her mouth. "You can dial 911 if I get food poisoning. Anyway, let me tell you about this great idea I just had. See, I was thinking about something I said to Mom last night about what a zombie she'd been lately and . . . "

"*Lexie . . . *"

"Just let me finish, Faith. Do you remember what I said to her? I said we'd been thinking about calling Rent-A-Parent for a replacement. I was just joking then, of course, but in school today, I happened to think about what I said, and it gave me this great idea for a way to make money and . . . "

"*Lexie!*"

Lexie scowled at her sister. "You don't have to scream like that, Faith. Just say what's on your mind and get it over with."

"Lexie, I'm trying to tell you something. Now shut up and listen. It's about Fido."

"Uh-oh," Lexie said. "What did he do? Did Mom catch him peeing on the furnace in the basement again?"

"No, it's nothing like that." Faith twisted her fingers together, and Lexie suddenly noticed that her sister's face was pale and anxious.

Her stomach tied itself into a tight hard knot in the middle of her body. "Is something wrong with Fido?" she asked in a small voice. "What happened to him?"

"Well, no one's sure. Daddy said Fido didn't come back home in the middle of the night the way he usually does, so early this morning he and Daniel went out to look for him. They found him sort of crawling around in the backyard. At first they thought he might be sick. But when they picked him up, they saw this great big bloody hole under one of his front legs."

Lexie sank down on one of the kitchen chairs. "Hole?" she repeated weakly. "Like from a cat fight?"

"Maybe," Faith said. "But Daddy thinks it was too big for that. He thinks Fido either got hit by a car or attacked by a big dog."

Lexie shut her eyes against the horrifying images of Fido's little body smacking against the side of a car or being torn to pieces by a giant Doberman. She took a deep breath and swallowed. She was afraid to ask any more questions, but still felt she had to know everything that had happened. "What . . . what did Daddy do with him?"

"He took him to the vet this morning on his way to work. I don't know what happened after that. When I got home from school, there wasn't anybody here. Not even Mom."

Lexie recalled that Bea Ware had been missing from her usual spot at the front curb. She frowned. "How come nobody told me about any of this in the morning?"

"Nobody could find you! What time did you leave for school, anyway?"

Lexie thought back to her unusually hurried breakfast. It seemed like an eternity had passed since she'd wolfed down her unappetizing piece of overdone toast and raced out the door. With a start, she realized she hadn't actually seen or spoken to anyone else in her family before she'd left the house.

"Do you think we could call Daddy at work or something?" she asked Faith. "Where's Mom, anyway? Except for meals and paying bills, this is the first time she's been out of the basement in weeks! Where do you suppose she could be?"

As if in answer to her question, footsteps sounded in the front hall. "This was the worst one yet, Frank," Mrs. Nielsen's voice was saying. "Everything was snarled up because of the snowstorm. And then to have that awful car give out on me right in the middle of that traffic jam!"

Mr. Nielsen said something in a low voice the girls couldn't hear.

51

"I'm not *saying* we should get a new car, Frank!" Mrs. Nielsen responded. "Don't you think I know that's out of the question? I'm merely venting my feelings about the car we *do* have, the car I'm *forced* to use for commuting to the university, the car which *seems* to have developed a personal antagonism toward me during a very stressful period in my life!"

By the end of her speech, Mrs. Nielsen's voice sounded slightly hysterical. Lexie and Faith looked at each other in dismay. Then they hurried into the living room.

"What happened, Daddy?" Lexie asked.

"Oh, old Bea pulled one of her usual tricks, and I had to leave work to rescue your mother from a gas station in the middle of nowhere. Fortunately, I'd just finished a meeting, so I was able to . . . "

"Not about *that*, Daddy!" Lexie interrupted. "What happened with Fido? What did the vet say?"

"Oh." Mr. and Mrs. Nielsen looked at each other and exchanged some sort of silent parental message. Mrs. Nielsen nodded and started out of the room. "Daddy's going to explain the situation to you and Faith, Lexie," she said over her shoulder. "I'm going to see if we have anything in the house for dinner."

Slowly, Mr. Nielsen unbuttoned his coat and pulled off his snowy woolen cap. "If you girls will sit down on the couch, I'll tell you what happened just as soon as

I put away these wet things." He went around the corner to the coat closet.

Without thinking, Lexie reached over and gripped her sister's hand. In complete silence, the two of them marched to the couch and sat down. Lexie steeled herself to hear the worst. She just knew it. Fido was dead, dead, dead.

"Fido's in bad shape," her father said, coming back around the corner and sinking into an armchair. "Dr. McManus, the vet, couldn't figure out what got hold of him, but she agreed it was a serious wound. Even so, she thinks there's a chance she might be able to patch him up with an operation."

Mr. Nielsen paused. Lexie and Faith both sat forward and stared at him, waiting for him to go on. Lexie noticed how tired her father looked.

"Of course," he continued, "the surgery is astronomically expensive. And even then Fido's recovery would be far from a certainty. Dr. McManus pointed out that it was only realistic to consider the possibility of having Fido put to sleep." Mr Nielsen ran a hand over his face. "I'm just sorry I let him out last night. And I did it against my better judgment, too."

Suddenly, Lexie couldn't stand to hear any more. She jumped to her feet and ran up the stairs to her room. There she threw herself onto her bed and curled up into a tiny ball. With her arms wrapped around her head, she concentrated on making her mind a total blank. Whenever a thought tried to enter her brain, she ground her teeth together and ferociously chased it away.

She had no idea how much time passed. Eventually, she must have fallen asleep. When she woke up, the room was completely dark. Her neck and shoulders were stiff and sore from sleeping in a balled-up position.

Painfully, she uncurled herself and stood up. Her first fuzzy thought was to go downstairs and get Fido, but then, with a jolt, she remembered. She ground her teeth together again, and tried to force the cat's image out of her mind. Thinking about Fido was torture and wouldn't do anybody any good.

She turned on the little lamp by her bed and peered at the dial on her Bugs Bunny clock. It was already 8:30. She'd slept right through dinner! She wondered why no one had come upstairs to get her. "Probably nobody noticed I was missing," she muttered out loud. "All alone and completely forgotten. As usual."

Still slightly groggy from her nap, she walked out into the hall and staggered into the tiny upstairs bathroom for a drink. Then she wandered back out into the hall again and stood there for a few minutes. Finally, she decided she might as well return to bed. But as she passed Faith's room, she heard a loud honking noise. She recognized it as the sound Faith made when she blew her nose. Lexie opened her sister's door and walked in.

Faith was sitting in the middle of her bed. She was clutching a small green and gold package. Her eyes were red and her face was swollen and puffy. She didn't even seem to notice that Lexie had come in without knocking.

Without saying anything, Lexie walked over and sat down next to her. For a long moment, the two sisters sat together in complete silence.

"They'll never pay for the operation, will they, Faith?" Lexie finally asked.

"I don't see how they *can!* Didn't you hear them with all the bills last night? And this afternoon about Bea Ware?"

"Yes. But what I don't understand is why things have gotten so much worse. Why are they *always* talking about money lately?"

"I'm not sure," Faith answered. "But I think it must be Karen's college. You know, she only got a partial scholarship, so they had to take out a loan to pay for the rest. I heard them talking, and they were saying things were going to be really tight till Mom gets her master's and can start earning some money again."

Lexie didn't say anything. Of course, she thought. Faith had to be right. Trust Karen to pick out one of the most expensive colleges in the whole country!

Because of that, there was no way her parents could afford to pay for an operation on a dumb old cat.

She sighed and pointed to the little package in Faith's hands. "Who's that for?"

"It . . . it's . . . f-f-for . . . " Faith's voice cracked, and she stopped speaking.

With a start, Lexie remembered the object she'd seen Faith wrapping in green and gold paper. "It's the catnip mouse," she whispered. "The one you got for Fido."

Faith nodded dumbly. All at once, Lexie felt as if her heart would break. Her eyes filled with hot tears. She buried her face in her hands and started crying. Her body shook with sobs.

"I was thinking," Faith said after a long while. "Maybe I might sleep in my old bed just for tonight. In your room."

Lexie sat up and stared at her sister through her tears. "Okay," she choked out. "But it's full of my junk."

"We'll just dump it all on the floor. The room's already so messy, nobody could tell the difference."

Lexie ignored the insult and got to her feet. Still weeping, she headed out the door. Faith followed her, and within a few minutes both of them were lying in their familiar positions in their old room. Lexie gave a shuddering sigh and pulled her blanket up under her chin. She'd stopped sobbing, but quiet tears still trickled down her cheeks. From across the room, she heard the soft sound of Faith breathing in and out, in and out.

Lexie had never felt more grateful for her sister's presence. She realized Faith hadn't given any reason for wanting to move back to her old bed. But Lexie didn't need a reason. It was enough to know that tonight of all miserable nights, she wouldn't have to be alone.

Eight

Mr. Nielsen woke Lexie up at five o'clock the next morning. When he turned on her bedside lamp and patted her shoulder, she let out a little scream of surprise and shot bolt upright in her bed. Confused and only half-awake, she stared around the room. To her tired, tear-swollen eyes, the gentle glow of the little lamp appeared as glaring as the light of the noonday sun. Outside the windows the winter sky loomed dark and threatening.

"It's bird census day!" Mr. Nielsen said cheerfully. "Rise and shine."

Lexie squinted at him, and her eyes ached even more. She gazed up at her father, and his image wavered and blurred. "Bird census day?" she repeated stupidly.

"You remember, Lexerino. The winter bird count. You said you wanted to come along. Now you need to scoot out of bed and get dressed. Come on! It'll take your mind off things."

"Don't make her go, Daddy." Faith was completely buried under her heavy quilt, and her voice came out a muffled, sleepy croak. "It's still the middle of the night. Give the little brat a break."

Startled at hearing Faith speaking from her old bed, Mr. Nielsen quickly turned to look in her direction. Just as quickly, he turned back to regard Lexie with wide, anxious blue eyes. "You don't want to come along? But the other night you seemed so eager to join me!"

Both Nielsen parents had the irritating habit of re-writing the past to suit their own purposes, and Lexie immediately recognized that this was what her father was doing. Normally, she would have argued with him, taking great pains to point out that she'd never said she wanted to go on the bird count, and that in fact she'd seemed the opposite of "eager" when he'd mentioned it. She knew she had logic, history, and even an eyewitness on her side. But this morning, she just didn't have the spirit for a fight.

"It doesn't matter," she said in a dull voice. "I might as well go."

Her father beamed and bounced out of the room. "I'll just go down and boil up some oatmeal while you're getting dressed," he called. "I'll put it in the thermos so we can eat while we drive. We don't want to lose any time."

Lexie let out a long, shuddering sigh and lurched to her feet. Bleary-eyed, she pawed through her dresser drawers, hunting for her warmest sweater, long underwear, and thick socks. The winter bird count never failed to take place on the coldest day of the year, and in Minnesota that was serious business. Miserable as she might feel, Lexie had no intention of freezing to death in her father's drafty old station wagon.

Fifteen minutes later, she was sitting in the front seat of the car, halfheartedly spooning lukewarm, lumpy oatmeal into her mouth. She radiated gloom. But her father was making a determined effort to be cheerful.

"Howsabout some riddles for the road, Lexerino? What's that old one we used to tell about the chicken with one arm?"

"I forget."

"Well, that's a first. Actually, I believe *I* remember it. Why did the chicken with one arm cross the road?"

"I don't *care,* Daddy."

"To get to the secondhand shop!" Mr. Nielsen chuckled and turned to grin at her. Lexie refused to meet his gaze. Instead, she licked her plastic spoon and screwed the top back on the thermos. Then she hunkered down in her seat and stared straight ahead at the glove compartment door.

But Mr. Nielsen wouldn't give up. "Omar Schwartz told me a great story at work the other day."

Lexie groaned inwardly. Mr. Schwartz's stories were famous for being long, boring, and not funny. She continued to stare straight ahead into the pre-dawn darkness, hoping her father would get the message and decide not to tell her the joke.

But Mr. Nielsen was undaunted. "It seems there was a reporter," he began, "who was sent to write a human interest story about a prison. The warden met him at the front gate and took him on a guided tour of the place. Well, the first thing the reporter noticed was the way the prisoners were banging their spoons against the bars of their cells. One of them would go, *Bang, bang, bang!* And then everybody else in the jail would break up laughing. Then another prisoner would go, *Bang, bang, bang,* bang! And everybody else would break up laughing again.

"Well, naturally, the reporter was curious. 'What does all that banging on the bars mean?' he asked the warden.

"The warden laughed. 'The whole jail memorized a

joke book a while back,' he explained. 'Now all the prisoners know the number of each joke. When they hear five knocks, they remember joke number five, and then they laugh. And so on.'

"Naturally, the reporter found this pretty hard to believe, so he decided to try it out for himself. On his way out, he asked one of the prisoners if he could borrow a spoon. Then the reporter took the spoon and started banging it against some cell bars. *Bang, bang, bang, bang, bang, bang!* he went.

"When he was finished, there was dead silence in the prison.'What gives?' the reporter asked the warden. 'Why didn't anybody laugh?'

"The warden shrugged and said, 'Well, you know how it is. Some people just don't know how to tell a good joke!' "

Mr. Nielsen threw back his head and guffawed at his story, but Lexie frowned in confusion. As usual, Mr. Schwartz's joke had made absolutely no sense to her. She turned to ask her father to explain it, but then she remembered she was trying not to be interested in anything that morning. She quickly turned her gaze back toward the glove compartment door.

Mr. Nielsen was quiet for a minute. "Well," he finally continued, "if it's too early in the morning for telling jokes, you might want to get out the Peterson and give it a onceover."

The "Peterson" was the birding guidebook Lexie's father carried everywhere with him, and Lexie knew it well. Whenever Mr. Nielsen was behind the wheel, he had the unsettling habit of suddenly veering over to the side of the road without any warning. He would then park, usually illegally, leap out of the car, and plunge into a nearby field or swamp to take bird pictures while the rest of the family waited for him. All the Nielsen children had been trained to use the Peterson guide to help identify any unusual species their father might come across in the wilderness by the roadside.

But now Lexie didn't even glance at the bird guide.

"I'm hoping to see some good birds today," Mr. Nielsen went on. "If we're lucky we'll get some pine siskins or some crossbills. Of course what I'd really like to spot is that snowy owl somebody reported seeing in the area. I've read there's a shortage of prey in the Arctic this year, so some of them have moved down here. . . . Of course, that's quite a long shot. But if I could report a snowy owl sighting when all the birders get together for the afternoon session, it would be a real feather in my cap!"

He chuckled and glanced sideways at Lexie to see if she'd caught his little pun. Lexie pulled up her collar and closed her eyes. Mr. Nielsen reached over and gave her arm a tentative pat. "Lexie, I know you're upset about the cat, and . . . "

"Forget it, Daddy." Lexie shook off her father's hand. "It doesn't matter. He's just a dumb old cat, and I don't want to talk about him."

Mr. Nielsen raised his eyebrows and started to speak, but just then he spotted the turnoff that led to the area he'd been assigned to count for the day. He slowed down and drove onto a bumpy, muddy dirt road that led back toward a patch of pine forest right next to an open snowy field. He came to a stop at the edge of the woods.

"Now here's my plan. I thought we'd hike along that trail over there." Mr. Nielsen pointed to a little path leading back through the pine trees. "We'll observe the back section of the woods for an hour or so till the sun is really up, and then we'll move forward and cover the front. How's that sound to you?"

"It sounds boring, Daddy. That's why I'm staying in the car."

"Don't be ridiculous, Lexie! You can't stay cooped up in the car all day."

"Want to make a bet?"

Mr. Nielsen didn't say anything for a long time. Even though she was carefully avoiding his gaze, Lexie knew exactly how her father's face looked at that moment. His expression would reveal a combination of exasperation, disappointment, and hurt feelings. Lexie felt a small pang of guilt at the nasty way she was treating him. She ground her teeth together so hard she forced the pang to disappear.

"All right, Lexie." When he spoke, her father's voice had lost all of its eager enthusiasm. The pang of guilt came back. This time, it was much bigger and stronger, and Lexie had a lot more trouble getting rid of it. "If you're determined not to have any fun on this expedition, you can at least make yourself useful."

Her father picked up the Peterson guide and opened it. "Your job can be to count the birds you see over there." He pointed to the big snowy field next to the pine woods. "Even though the sun's not really up yet, I can already see some horned larks. They look like this. They're pretty common, but we still have to count them."

Slowly, Lexie turned her head and looked over at an illustration of a little brown-and-white bird with a yellow-and-black face. She opened her mouth and gave an exaggerated yawn.

Mr. Nielsen sighed and handed her a pad and pencil. "Make a slash mark on the paper whenever you see one. Horned larks are usually in big flocks, so you may have to do some fast counting. If you see any other birds you don't recognize, try to find them in the Peterson. Then you can record them also." He gathered up his binoculars, camera, and tripod. Then he glanced at his watch. "I'll try to be back in an hour."

He got out of the car and slammed the door without even bothering to say good-bye. Lexie blinked in surprise. Her father was so good-natured it was usually pretty difficult to push him into acting rude. The pang of guilt returned again, and this time it was there to stay.

Lexie groaned and stretched her arms up over her head. What am I doing here at the crack of dawn? she asked herself. What was I thinking of when I said I'd come along? It wouldn't have been hard to get out of this stupid trip!

Lexie knew she could easily have said she was sick or had too much homework or something. But *noooo*. She'd been too sleepy and depressed to think of any good excuses. So instead she'd said it didn't matter. And now here she was, stuck in this boring, freezing car for the rest of the day. With nothing to do but think about poor Fido, lying in the cold, hard corner of a hospital cage, wounded, or worse yet, dying or maybe even already . . .

"No!" she said out loud. She *wasn't* going to think about Fido. Anything would be better than that! Even birds!

Hastily, she grabbed up the Peterson and her pad and pencil and got out of the car. When she closed the door, a flock of birds rose up from the open field next to the forest. Lexie recognized them as the horned larks her father had shown her in the book. "Whoa!" she yelled. "How am I supposed to count all those?"

She stared up at the low-flying birds, noticing their black tailfeathers and counting as fast as she could. As she did, she listened to the high-pitched tinkling sound of the larks' call. She had to admit they were pretty—even if they *were* common.

She wrote down a number and walked a little closer to the field. Another large flock of birds rose up at her approach. "Uh-oh," Lexie said out loud. "You guys are different."

She opened the Peterson and frantically pawed through the pages, looking for a picture that resembled the little brown, white, and gray birds she could see in the air. Nothing looked right. But finally, near the very end of the book, she thought she'd found it.

"Snow buntings," she read. "Often seen with horned larks. Has notable white wing patches." She peered up at the birds in flight. "Hey! Hot dog! You guys *do* have white wing patches!" She started counting again and wrote another number on her pad. When she was finished, she realized she was panting with excitement. For the first time in her life, she began to understand why her father loved birding so much.

Flushed with her success at identifying the snow buntings, she crossed the snowy ground toward the field. The early morning wind whipped her face and her eyes began to tear and sting. She stuffed her book and papers into the pockets of her parka and put on her heavy mittens. Then she pulled up her hood and snapped it under her chin. She'd give the birds one more minute, she decided. Then she was getting back in the car.

Slowly, she moved even closer to the stubbly field. She shielded her eyes with her hand and peered ahead of her. Had something moved out there by that rotten stump? The early morning sun was just coming up, and it was difficult to see anything in the pale gray light. But even so, Lexie was sure she'd seen the flicker of a shadow on the snow by the old stump.

She took a few steps to the right and then carefully approached the field again. She came to a stop at the very outside edge of the forest. Once again, she stared out at the stump. A sharp gust of freezing wind blasted her in the face. She shivered and decided to go back to the car. But just as she turned to leave, another fleeting movement caught her eye. Lexie turned back and peered out at the field one more time. Then she caught her breath. The biggest bird she'd ever seen in her life was standing on the ground right next to the stump! The reason the bird was so hard to see was that it was pure white.

The creature was almost two feet tall and had a round smooth head and huge black talons partially covered with downy white feathers that looked like fur. With a thudding of her heart, Lexie realized what she was looking at. The giant bird *had* to be a snowy owl! She *had* to get her father! As slowly as she could force herself to move, she backed away from the field. Then she plunged into the woods and hurtled along the path her father had taken.

"Daddy!" she cried softly. "Daddy! Daddy, come here!"

She crashed into her father halfway into the forest. He was rushing back along the path in her direction. "Lexie!" he exclaimed, grabbing both her shoulders. "I heard you calling. What's the matter? What happened? Are you all right?"

"I saw it, Daddy! I saw it! In the field!"

"You saw *what?*"

"The owl. The snowy owl!"

Her father caught his breath. "Are you sure? What does it look like?" As he spoke, Mr. Nielsen started back along the path that led out of the woods.

"Well, it's huge," Lexie said breathlessly. "And it's almost all white. And it's got big black claws for feet. And it's just standing there!"

Unable to control himself, Mr. Nielsen broke into a trot. Lexie ran to keep up with him. When they reached the edge of the woods, they both slowed down to a painfully careful walk. As they approached the field, Lexie prayed the owl would still be there. At first, as they came around the edge of the trees, she couldn't see it, and she was sure it had flown away. But then, as she gazed ahead, she saw that the owl was still standing in the very same spot in the middle of the field.

"There it is, Daddy," she whispered in her father's ear. "Out there by that stump."

Her father looked out across the snow, and an expression of intense delight came over his face. With one arm, he hugged Lexie's shoulders. Then he got down on his hands and knees and crawled across the snowy, frozen ground toward the field. When he was just a few yards away from the owl, he slithered to a stop and began fiddling with his camera and tripod. At the very instant Mr. Nielsen finally got his equipment ready, the owl stepped out of the shadow into the full sunlight.

Lexie couldn't believe it. It was almost as if the owl were posing to have his picture taken! And what an incredible picture he made. The bird's feathers gleamed in the pale winter light. Except for a few speckles of blackish brown, he was almost completely white. He looked so soft and smooth in the sunshine, Lexie wished she could reach out and touch him. Because she'd been the first one to discover him, she felt as if the owl were *hers* somehow.

When she was sure her father had had time to take at least a thousand pictures, she couldn't help walking closer to the field to get a better look. Finally, she was only a few feet behind him. As she approached the stump, the owl turned his round head in her direction.

His eyes widened, and Lexie gasped. The owl was staring right at her! His hooked, sharp beak was obviously capable of ripping a mouse to shreds, but his broad, high forehead gave him a look of great wisdom, kindness, and insight. As she stared back at him, Lexie felt as if the bird could somehow read all her thoughts and feelings and was trying to send her a silent, urgent message. With a painful start of recognition, she realized what that all-knowing yellow gaze reminded her of. The snowy owl's eyes looked just like Fido's!

She gave another little gasp, and the owl took off into the air. As he rose up above her, Lexie watched his huge wings open so wide they blocked out the morning sun. She was dimly aware of the clicking sound of the camera as her father continued snapping picture after picture.

When the owl was a distant dot in the sky, Mr. Nielsen jumped to his feet and ran toward her. "How about that, Lexie? How about that? And I thought *I* was the birder in the family."

To her father's amazement, Lexie burst into tears and threw her arms around his waist. "Please, Daddy," she sobbed. "Please say it's not too late! Please say Fido can have the operation!"

"But, Lexie, I—"

"I'll help pay for it! I don't have any money now, but I know I can earn some. I have an idea for some jobs I can get, and I just know I can earn some money. Please, let's go to a phone right now and call the vet and tell her to operate before it's too late."

Through her thick parka, Lexie could feel her father patting her on the back. "Lexie," he said. "Lexie. No wonder you've been so upset. You and I seem to have had a real communication breakdown here."

Lexie pulled back far enough to stare up into her father's eyes. The cruel wind lashed at her wet face, but she hardly noticed. "Communication breakdown?" she repeated.

"Yes, indeed." Mr. Nielsen gently pushed her back toward the car. "You see, I told Dr. McManus to go ahead with the surgery yesterday when I took Fido in!"

Lexie's mouth dropped open. "You did?"

"Of course I did! Why, I'm just as fond of the old boy as you are, Lexie. I thought we should at least *try* to save him."

Lexie sobbed even harder. "But—but—you said the operation would be so expensive, I thought . . . Faith and I thought . . . "

"Oh, dear. I guess it's pretty obvious I didn't explain things as clearly as I'd meant to yesterday. I thought you girls understood I'd authorized the surgery! When you rushed out of the room like that, I thought it was because you were worried Fido might die anyway, and needed some time by yourself. And later, when Mom checked on you in your room, she said you were sound asleep. Neither one of us had the heart to wake you up."

"So you didn't forget about me?"

"Lexie, your parents may be a little scatty from time to time, but I don't believe we're *completely* hopeless yet!"

Her father opened the car door and Lexie climbed inside. She was still shuddering and sobbing uncontrollably. "Dry your face before it freezes, Lexerino," he told her. He walked around to the other side and got in the car himself. Then he reached down and picked up a thermos bottle. Lexie looked at it and made a face.

"I d-d-don't want any more oatmeal, Daddy," she said through her tears.

"It's not oatmeal. This one has hot chocolate in it." Her father unscrewed the top and filled it with the steaming brown liquid. "Careful. It's still piping hot. Don't burn yourself."

He handed Lexie her drink. Then he pulled another thermos out from under his seat and poured himself a mug full of coffee. He took a big swallow and shook his head. "I'm really sorry about this mix-up, kiddo," he said. "I guess your mother and I have had so much on our minds these days, what with Karen's college costs and then the car breaking down like that yesterday . . . "

"And don't forget Mom's thesis."

"Oh, right. Heaven forbid we'd forget Mom's thesis!" Mr. Nielsen made a wry face and then drank some more coffee. "But back to the issue at hand, what I'm trying to say is that, what with all these other things going on lately, it's just possible your mother and I haven't been as tuned in to you kids and your problems as usual." He patted Lexie on the knee. "But that doesn't mean we're not aware you've been going through a rough patch, Lexerino. Even Mom has noticed, thesis and all. Having your best friend move away is not an easy thing. And now, what with Fido being hurt . . . "

A fresh set of tears started down Lexie's cheeks. "I just feel so lonely all the time, Daddy!" she sobbed. "I don't have anybody to do things with anymore or talk to or anything! Fido was the last friend I had left, and now he's . . . he might be . . . "

Mr. Nielsen pulled a large white handkerchief out of his pocket and handed it to her. "It's not an easy thing," he said again. "And it's not always easy to make new friends, either, particularly not good ones like Debby."

"You can say that again," Lexie said through her tears.

"That again." Mr. Nielsen gently patted her shoulder. "It's not always easy to make new friends. And sometimes we simply have to face the cold, hard fact that occasionally we're going to be stuck with nobody but Me, Myself, and I for companions."

Mr. Nielsen looked out the window for a minute. "But do you want to know something strange, Lexerino?" he went on. "I've come to place an extremely high value on the hours I spend alone! Mind you, I'm not saying I'd want to be alone all the time, like a hermit. But, to be honest, I think the chance to be alone is the main reason I enjoy birding so much. It's a great excuse to go off by myself . . . alone, but *with* Me, Myself, and I!"

Lexie giggled through her tears. "That sounds kind of nuts, Daddy. Do you talk to You, Yourself, and You, too?"

Mr. Nielsen laughed. "Well, sometimes I do. Frankly, Me and I don't have much to say to one another. But Myself is a pretty darned good conversationalist."

Lexie laughed out loud. Then her face grew serious again. "Did you ever have a best friend move away?"

"To be sure. More than once, in fact. By the time you get to be an old codger like me, Lex, you realize that people are always moving in and out of your life in one way or another. Why, just look at our family these days! Karen's moved away to college, and we all miss her. Mom's semi-moved into the basement, and we all miss her. And Faith's moved out of your room, and now you two miss each other."

Lexie choked on a mouthful of hot chocolate, and her father grinned. "Come on, admit it, Lexerino. I saw Faith in her old bed this morning."

"Oh, *I* might admit it. But Faith never would."

75

"You're probably right about that." Mr. Nielsen drank some more coffee. "But I guess my point is that, even though the people in our family are moving all around these days, we're still a family. Just the way you and Debby are still friends, even though you don't live in the same town anymore."

"It sort of reminds me of my jigsaw puzzles," Lexie said thoughtfully. "The people are like a bunch of pieces. Most of the time, everybody's spilled out all over my closet floor. But you can still stick us back together again and make the same old picture."

"Not a bad analogy, Lexie," her father said. "Quite poetic, in fact. Except that I like to think we're not as messy as your closet floor. *Nothing* is as messy as your closet floor!"

Lexie giggled again and then hiccupped out one last sob. "What you said before about Fido is true, isn't it, Daddy? He might still die even if he does have the surgery?"

Her father nodded. "I'm afraid that is a real possibility. Your mother was planning to call the animal hospital this morning to find out how things went. By the time we get home, we ought to have some news about Fido's progress."

Lexie sniffled and drank some more hot chocolate. "Either way," she said, "I do still want to help pay for the operation."

"I appreciate the offer, Lexie. I'll accept any contributions you want to make." He looked out at the open field and frowned as the wind dashed a few icy snowflakes against the windshield. "I think we're about to be hit with another big storm. We'd better get going before we're stranded out here." He turned the key in the ignition and set the heater on high. "Besides," he added as he turned the car around, "after that snowy owl, I don't care if I see another bird for the rest of the day!"

"He was really unbelievable, wasn't he? I'm never going to forget seeing *him!*"

Lexie finished her cup of hot chocolate and snuggled down in her seat. After a long, sleepy pause, she said, "Daddy, when the going gets tough, what can you *always* count on?"

Mr. Nielsen looked over at her and smiled. "Your father? Your family?"

"No! Your *fingers!* You can always count on your *fingers!*"

Now it was Mr. Nielsen's turn to frown in confusion. "It's number four, Daddy," Lexie explained. She leaned forward and tapped her plastic spoon on the dashboard. *Bang, bang, bang, bang.* "You know. It's a *joke!*"

Her father rolled his eyes at her, but then he laughed out loud. After that, he turned onto the main road and headed for home.

Nine

By the time Lexie and her father pulled into the garage at home, several inches of snow had already fallen. Mrs. Nielsen met them at the top of the basement steps. "You're back early," she said. "Think of all those poor birds left uncounted."

"True," said Mr. Nielsen. "But wait until you hear about the bird we *did* see. Lexie discovered a full-blown mature snowy owl!"

"That's fantastic! And to think the two of you saw it together. What a lovely bonding experience." Lexie's mother clapped her hands together and danced a little jig on the tile floor.

Lexie and her father eyed her suspiciously. "Mom, are you okay?" Lexie asked. "I don't remember you ever getting that excited about a bird before!"

Her mother laughed. "Well, I do have some other reasons for being cheerful," she admitted. "I have two pieces of good news of my own. The first one is that, despite the odds, Fido survived his surgery and seems to be holding his own. If he continues to improve, they think he'll be able to come home before Christmas!"

"Hooray!" Lexie screamed at the top of her lungs. "Thank you, Mom! Thank you, Daddy! Thank you, Dr. McManus!"

"We'll have to be careful with him, though," her mother warned. "We'll have to change his bandages and give him medicine and keep him inside no matter how much he begs to go out."

"I'll make him a bed in my room."

"He'll never get better in *that* pigsty!" put in Faith, who'd just returned from her baby-sitting job. "The cooties under Lexie's bed will give poor Fido an infection! You'd better let me take care of him instead."

"Just shut up, Faith!" Lexie began. "Why do you always have to be such a big, fat—"

"Girls!" Mr. Nielsen shut the basement door with a bang. "Be quiet! I want to hear your mother's other piece of good news!"

79

Faith and Lexie looked at Mrs. Nielsen. She looked back at them, grinning enormously.

"Mom," Lexie said impatiently, "what *is* it!"

"Well . . . I finished my thesis!"

"Hooray!" This time, Mr. Nielsen was the one who shouted. When everyone stared at him, his face turned bright red. "Uh . . . ," he mumbled. "That is to say, congratulations, my dear. I'm sure your advisors at the university will recognize the brilliance of your work."

"They'd better," Mrs. Nielsen said darkly. "After all the time I put in on that thing."

"You can say that again," said Faith. "Now just how soon can you start earning big bucks counseling psychopaths, Mom?"

Lexie opened her mouth to say, "You mean like *you,* Faith?" but the mention of "bucks" reminded her of her plan for earning money for Christmas shopping and Fido's operation. So instead of starting a fight, she left the kitchen and ran upstairs to her room. There she hauled three big pieces of leftover poster board from the back of her closet. She got out her scissors and cut each one of them in half. After that, she began the hunt for her Magic Markers, which she finally found scattered on the floor under her bed. At last, she sat down in the middle of the rug and got to work.

Twenty minutes later, she went downstairs. She was carrying six posters. This is what they said:

NEED A JOB DONE?
Then why not...

RENT - A - KID

- Snow Shoveling
- Dog Walking
- Fish Feeding
- Plant Watering
  and more....

NO JOB TOO SMALL! REASONABLE RATES!!

call: LEXIE NIELSEN · 555-4225

She found her father in a darkened corner of the living room. He was listening to an opera while carefully unloading the film from his camera.

"I can't wait to get these developed, Lexie," he told her. "If they turn out, I'm sure we'll have something worth entering in the Audubon photography contest."

"That's great, Daddy. Can I borrow the hammer and some nails?"

"Sure, Lexie. They're downstairs in the garage. Just be sure you return the hammer when you're finished."

Lexie put on her damp parka and scampered down the stairs to the basement. She went out to her father's toolbox, where she found the hammer and a handful of nails. Then she left the house through the garage door and hurried back out into the storm.

Half an hour later, she was home again. Her cheeks were flushed with cold and excitement. "Guess what, Faith?" she announced as she burst into the kitchen. "I already have two snow-shoveling jobs. Mrs. Fisher and some other lady saw me putting up my posters outside and told me to come over as soon as it stops snowing, and . . . "

"Quiet, Lexie!" Faith snarled at her. "Can't you see I'm on the phone?" She spoke into the receiver. "You'll have to say that again, Karen. Some loudmouth just started talking to me, and I couldn't hear you. Wait a minute. I'll write it down. Your plane gets in tomorrow morning at 9:32—*not* tomorrow afternoon at 12:06? Okay, I'll tell Mom and Daddy."

Faith listened in silence for a minute. Then she cleared her throat. "There is one thing I wanted to ask you about, Karen. About your room—*my* room, I mean, I was wondering—" She stopped speaking and listened again. "You did? Really? No! I don't think we ever got it! That's just terrific. That's really nice of you, Karen. Well, of course you can understand how I feel. I mean, we all know how messy Lexie is and . . .

you have to go now? Okay! See you tomorrow!"

She hung up the phone and turned to grin at Lexie, who was standing in the middle of the kitchen glowering at her. "Guess what, Lexie? Karen says she wrote a letter a long time ago saying she'd sleep down in the basement while she's home for vacation. Do you think Mom got it and forgot to tell me about it? But anyway, the important thing is that I won't have to move back in with you!"

"That's just fine with me! You snored so loud last night I hardly got any sleep."

Faith made a face at her. "What were you blabbing about when you came in before, anyway?"

"Oh, right. I was just outside putting up my new Rent-A-Kid posters, and two different people asked me to come shovel their walks!"

Faith snorted. "Now isn't that bitterly ironic? The kid who'll never shovel her *own* family's walk is planning to take money for shoveling *other* people's! Do these customers of yours know what a terrible shoveler you are? Do they know your habit of quitting halfway through any job you start?"

With a growl of rage, Lexie lunged across the kitchen and grabbed her sister's shoulders. She was reaching up to yank out a handful of Faith's bushy brown hair when the phone rang again. Faith pushed her away and reached for the receiver.

"Hello? Who? Oh, you want to talk to *her*. Well, if you're *sure* . . . " She handed the receiver to Lexie and strolled out of the room.

Lexie scowled after her. How, she asked herself, could her father *possibly* believe she and Faith would *ever* miss each other? She worked hard to swallow her anger. When she spoke into the phone, her voice came out a breathless gasp. "Hello?"

"Hi! It's me!"

"Hi, Me!" Lexie immediately recognized her friend Debby's soft, gentle voice. She smiled and sat down on the kitchen floor, hugging the telephone receiver with both hands. "Why haven't you written in so long?"

"Why haven't *I* written? What are you talking about? You owe me two letters!"

Lexie looked puzzled. "Really? You know, I'm beginning to think something's going on with the mailman around here. Nobody's been getting any letters lately!"

"Ahhhh. The Mystery of the Missing Mail."

Lexie giggled. "The Secret of the Lost Letters."

"The Case of the Evaporating Envelopes. The Curse of the Vanishing . . . oops! My mom's yelling at me to make it short. So what's new, anyway? How are Suzy and Cheryl?"

"Oh, them. I never even see Suzy anymore. And Cheryl's a whole new person these days." As she spoke, she remembered she'd never found out what Cheryl's "urgently important" message for her was. She reminded herself to track Cheryl down at school on Monday and find out why her friend had written that note.

"So what else is new?"

"Oh, everything. You wouldn't believe all the stuff that's been going on." In a rush of words, Lexie poured out the stories of Fido, the snowy owl, and her new Rent-A-Kid business.

"Wow!" Debby exclaimed when she'd finished. "I'm sure glad Tabby-Fido's going to get better. I'm glad I didn't know he was hurt, or I would have been worried to death! You must have been scared stiff."

Lexie's eyes filled with tears. "I really was," she said in a shaky voice.

Debby was quiet for a few seconds, but Lexie could feel her silent sympathy traveling along the phone wires. "What's happening with that new girl?" she asked at last. "You know, the one you wrote me about who thinks she's so great? Tara Lynch-Harrison?"

Lexie giggled again. "You mean Tarantula Lynch-Harrison? Well, actually, I think I've finally managed to get even with her." She described her witch drawing in detail and told how she'd left it in Tara's desk. Then she leaned back against the cupboard door and waited for Debby to laugh.

But the laugh never came. Instead, her friend's gentle voice sounded worried. "Don't you think that might really hurt her feelings, Lex?"

Lexie frowned in irritation at Debby's lack of

understanding and support. But when she answered, she tried to use a casual, offhand tone. "Well, now that you mention it, I suppose it wasn't exactly the nicest thing in the world to do. But Tara deserves it, doesn't she? After all, you've never met her, Debby. If you could just see her parading all over the place flipping her hair around, you'd understand what I'm talking about."

"I *guess* so."

"Believe me, you would, Debby. She's really just awful!" Lexie spoke in a loud, emphatic voice that echoed and jangled inside her head. As she listened to herself in dismay, she realized the subject of Tara Lynch-Harrison was beginning to make her feel nervous and uncomfortable. She decided it was time to talk about something else. "So what's going on in California, anyway? Do you have blonde hair yet?"

Debby, who had brown hair so dark it was almost black, snorted. For the next few minutes, she chattered on about her new school. She told several funny stories about California customs like kids having their lockers on the outside of the school buildings and teachers calling a light rain a "winter storm." By the time Mrs. Figenbaum kicked Debby off the phone, Lexie had completely forgotten about Tara.

But she hadn't forgotten about the Mystery of the Missing Mail. After she hung up the phone, she left the kitchen and stalked into the living room. There, she went to the wall by the front door and opened the glass door to the mail chute. As usual, the little square box was empty.

"Hmmmm," she said out loud. "Very interesting." She got down on her hands and knees and tried to peer up into the chute. All she could see was blackness. But when she wedged her hand up inside the narrow space, the tips of her fingers touched the very bottom edge of a thick, solid wad of paper.

"Aha!" she cried. She ran back into the kitchen and started pawing through drawers, hunting for the right tool. At last, she discovered the long wooden-handled tongs her father used when he barbecued hamburgers in the summer. She grabbed them and hurried back into the living room. She bent down and poked the tongs up the mail chute.

It took several tries, but she finally managed to latch on to the edge of the wad of paper. Slowly and carefully she pulled downward. At first, the paper seemed to be jammed tight. But finally, the wad came loose. It shot straight down and landed with a thump. A huge pile of magazines and envelopes spilled out onto the floor.

"Oh, my goodness!" her mother cried as she and Faith came around the corner into the living room. "Look at all those bills we haven't been paying."

"Hey!" exclaimed Faith, scooping up letters from the

floor. "Here are Daniel's missing *Sports Illustrated*s. And here's Karen's letter saying I don't have to move out of my room!"

Mrs. Nielsen sat down on the floor and started sorting through the pile. "There are two letters for you, Lexie. Both from California. From the postmarks, it looks like that wad has been stuck up there for at least two weeks. But we have been getting *some* mail, haven't we? I'm sure we would have noticed if we weren't getting any at all. Which means some of it must have been slipping down from time to time just to fool us. Or else I've been in more of a thesis fog than I thought I was!" She picked up a bill from the gas company and sighed. "What made you decide to investigate, anyway, Lexie? Lexie?"

Her youngest daughter didn't answer. In fact, Lexie didn't even realize her mother was speaking to her. She was too distracted by the letter she was holding. It was small and bright red, and it was addressed to her. From its size and color, she knew it had to be a party invitation. The date on the postmark was a week and a half old. The name on the return address was Tara Lynch-Harrison's.

Ten

By the time she was halfway through her first snow-shoveling job the next day, Lexie began to have second thoughts about her Rent-A-Kid business. Almost a foot of snow had fallen overnight, and it was wet and dense. Each shovelful felt heavier than the one before, and Lexie's back was already aching from her efforts. After one particularly weighty load, she straightened up and gazed thoughtfully at the house behind her. Mrs. Fisher was such a nice old lady, she told herself. She'd understand if Lexie told her the job was just too big for a ten-year-old.

Lexie stuck her shovel into a snowbank and started up toward the house. But before she'd taken two steps, she remembered Faith sneering at her in the kitchen the day before, telling her what a quitter she was. Abruptly, Lexie stopped and turned around. She picked up the shovel and went back to work.

"I am," she said out loud, "a lean, mean snow-blowing machine." Then she began singing "There's No Business Like Snow Business." She shoveled to the rhythm of the song, hoisting a shovelful over her head every time she sang the word "snow."

She sang to help with the work. But she also sang for another reason. She hoped it would help her avoid thinking about Tara Lynch-Harrison opening her desk and finding that awful witch drawing in school the next day. But loud as she sang, she still couldn't keep the image out of her mind. Finally, she decided to have a conversation with Me, Myself, and I.

"There's nothing you can do about it today anyway, dummy," Me told her, "so stop worrying about it all the time."

"Right," echoed I. "All you have to do is get to school early tomorrow and sneak the picture back out of Tara's desk. It's as simple as that. So just stop thinking about it!"

"Okay," Lexie said. "I'll try to think about something else."

"But look at the scraggly shadow of your hair on the snow," said Myself. "Doesn't it look just like the witch's hair?"

"Now that you mention it," said Me, "the snow shovel looks like the witch's broom, too."

"And what about that patch of ice on the sidewalk?" said I. "Doesn't it remind you of the witch's ice skates?"

"Quiet, you three!" Lexie yelled. "You're no help at all!"

She gave herself herself an angry shake and rang the bell to ask for her money.

"What about the back walk?" Mrs. Fisher asked when she opened the door. "Did you forget about that?"

Lexie gave her a blank look. "You wanted me to do the back walk?"

Mrs. Fisher nodded. "I distinctly remember asking you to shovel both the front *and* the back walks. I need that path cleared so I can get out to my bird feeders."

"I guess I didn't hear you." Lexie turned around and picked up her shovel again. "Sorry."

"Don't apologize, dearie," Mrs. Fisher said as she closed the door. "These little communication breakdowns happen from time to time. They're nothing to worry about."

"Communication breakdowns." As she wearily

dragged her shovel around to the back of the house, the words echoed in Lexie's head. *Communication breakdowns.*

Lately, it seemed as if her life had been *filled* with communication breakdowns! With Faith, with her mother, with her father before the bird census . . . and finally, because of the stopped-up mail chute, her family had had a communication breakdown with the entire outside world!

"If I'd gotten that party invitation when I was supposed to, I'd never have put that witch in Tara's desk," Lexie said out loud. "I'm in a big fat mess, and it isn't even my fault!"

"Not really." Me, Myself, and I all spoke at once. "The truth is that putting that witch in Tara's desk was a really babyish thing to do. The truth is that it's Tara's party, and she has the right to invite whoever she wants to!"

Lexie groaned and bashed her shovel against the sidewalk. Listening to the truth was hard. To quiet the nagging voices in her mind, she opened her mouth and started singing her Snow Business song again. Within a few minutes, she'd shoveled the entire back walk.

"You do excellent work, young lady," Mrs. Fisher said when Lexie rang the front doorbell for a second time. "Can I sign you up as my regular shoveler?" She handed Lexie a small pile of bills.

"I guess so." Lexie took the money and pressed her

hand against the small of her aching back. She remembered she'd already agreed to shovel a whole other walk that day. "But you know, I do other jobs besides shoveling, too. Dog walking, plant watering, bird and fish feeding while you're on vacation . . . "

"I'm not going anywhere!" Mrs. Fisher chuckled. "I went to Florida once and thought it was the most boring place in the world. Give me a good, solid Minnesota winter anytime." She waggled a finger at Lexie. "You just come on back next time it snows, young lady. I can keep you in business till next spring!"

"Okay." Lexie thanked Mrs. Fisher for the money and said good-bye. As she strolled back down the neatly shoveled walk, she realized she really had done a good job. She decided she'd earned a rest and a quick snack before she went on to her next house.

When she got home, her father was just pulling the station wagon into the driveway. Before he'd even come to a full stop, Lexie's sister Karen had thrown open the car door and jumped out. "Lex-Lex!" she screamed. "I can't believe it! You've grown a foot since I left!"

"Does that mean I have three feet now?" Lexie asked. "Do I have a whole yard?" As she spoke, she ran up to the car and hugged her sister.

"Oh, you and your silly jokes!" Karen hugged her back and kissed the top of her forehead. "I guess you haven't changed that much after all!"

"Well, you sure have!" Lexie stared up at Karen. In

fact, her sister looked like a different person. She'd let her trim short hair grow long, and now it stood out around her head in a wild, frizzy circle. Instead of the neat wool skirt and sweater she'd always worn in high school, she had on a baggy sweatshirt and jeans with holes in the knees. Long silver earrings dangled from her ears. "You look a *lot* better!"

Karen squealed. "Well, thank you, Lex-Lex! Now come on and help me carry my things inside." She reached into the car and pulled out three suitcases. She handed the heaviest one to Lexie. "Now be careful with that. Carry it directly into the basement and leave it by the couch. Gently lay it down on its side with the buckles facing up. *Don't* open it. And then come straight back to the car so you can carry something else."

Lexie picked up the suitcase and smiled ruefully. Karen might look different on the outside, she thought. But she hadn't changed on the inside.

"It's the old jigsaw pieces all over again," she said as she dutifully dragged the heavy suitcase into the basement. "And the biggest, bossiest part of the picture just fit right back into her place in the family puzzle!"

She deposited the suitcase and started up the stairs. On the way, she could hear her whole family chattering in the living room. They were telling Karen the local news and trying to find out what was happening at college, all at the same time. Everybody sounded so excited and happy that Lexie could hardly wait to go in and join them.

But then she remembered her next snow-shoveling job. She groaned out loud and glanced out the back window at the grim gray sky. Maybe she wouldn't go. After all, she didn't really *know* the second person who'd asked her to shovel.

She paused by the top of the basement steps, listening to the cheerful conversation in the living room. As she considered what to do, a sunbeam shone right into her eyes and she realized she was standing on Fido's mat. With a rush of feeling she remembered how her poor broke parents had agreed to pay for her pet's operation. All at once, she knew she didn't want to shut down her Rent-A-Kid company on its very first day.

She closed the basement door behind her and tromped across the kitchen floor in her boots, depositing little clumps of dirty snow as she went. Then she pulled on her mittens, snapped her hood, and went back outside into the cold air.

Eleven

The next morning, Lexie set a new speed record for getting to school. In fact, she got there so early the building wasn't even open, and she had to stand outside stomping her feet and clapping her hands together to keep from freezing. While she waited, she continually shot nervous glances over her shoulder, desperately hoping not to see Tara sauntering down the walk in her direction.

The instant the principal unlocked the big front doors, Lexie scurried inside and ran up the stairs to her classroom. Unfortunately, Mr. Lange wasn't as prompt as she was. Once again, Lexie was forced to wait several long, agonizing minutes in the hallway outside the locked classroom door. When she finally saw her teacher strolling along the corridor jingling his keys in his pocket, she felt as if she were on the verge of a nervous breakdown.

"Get a move on!" she wanted to shout. Instead, she gave Mr. Lange an anxious little smile.

But her teacher was in no hurry to open the door. When he saw Lexie, he grinned and walked up to her. "Top of the morning to you, Señorita Nielsen!" he boomed.

He leaned his broad back up against some lockers and started chatting. As he spoke, he slowly drew his key ring out of his pocket and began fiddling with it. "What makes you such an early bird today?"

Normally, Lexie loved joking around with Mr. Lange and would have tried to invent a worm pun as a response to his early bird question. But today her sense of humor had deserted her. She had to fight not to scream at him. "Uh . . . uh . . . I . . . um . . . thought I'd catch up on my math homework."

Mr. Lange clapped her on the shoulder with one of his huge hands. "*Magnifico! Stupendo!* You know, if you'd just spend a little more time with Mr. Math, he could be a good friend of yours. He doesn't have to be the archenemy you make him out to be."

Lexie faked another smile and stared pointedly at the key ring which was now looped over one of Mr. Lange's sausage fingers. Her teacher noticed her glance and winked at her. Then he bent down to put the key into the lock. At the same instant, Lexie saw Tara Lynch-Harrison come around the corner at the far end of the hallway.

Slowly, slowly, the key turned halfway around in the lock. Then it got stuck. Mr. Lange muttered under his breath, kicked the door and violently jiggled the door-knob. After an eternity, the key turned the rest of the way around.

By the time Mr. Lange finally pulled open the door, Lexie was in a frenzy of impatience. When the teacher started to walk into the room, Lexie stepped in front of him and squeezed through the tiny opening between his body and the door frame. She knew Mr. Lange was staring at her as she hurried toward Tara's desk, but she couldn't worry about that now. She just didn't have the time.

She darted down the aisle to the back row. Then she yanked open the top of Tara's desk. She was just closing it again when Tara walked into the room. Lexie quickly put her hand behind her back and crumpled the witch drawing into a ball.

"Hi, Lexie!" Tara's enormous blue eyes were bewildered. "What were you doing in my desk?"

Lexie's cheeks flamed, but when she spoke, her voice

sounded almost normal. "I was putting in a note. Saying I can come to your holiday party."

Tara flashed her dazzling white smile and casually swept a stray curl off her forehead. She opened her desk and took out the hastily scrawled message Lexie had written on a piece of notebook paper at breakfast that morning. As she did, Lexie saw a little glob of grape jelly stuck to the bottom corner of the note. Her cheeks burned even hotter, but Tara didn't seem to notice.

"Well, this solves a mystery for me, Lexie. The other day Cheryl *demanded* to know why I hadn't invited you to my party, and I told her she was bananas! Of *course* I invited Lexie to my party, I told her. Absolutely *everybody* is coming to my party, Cheryl, I said!"

Lexie felt her mouth dropping open in surprise, and she quickly snapped it shut. Guiltily, she remembered how she hadn't paid any attention to Cheryl's "Urgently important" message last week. Once again, the words "communication breakdown" sounded and resounded in her mind. And there was no question about whose fault this breakdown was. Cheryl might have changed, Lexie thought guiltily, but she was still nice enough to stick up for her old friend. And Lexie hadn't even bothered to answer her note.

"Well, anyway, I'm thrilled you can come, Lexie!" Tara's enthusiastic words broke in on her thoughts. "Do you know, you are the absolute last person I've heard from? Every single other kid in the class said yes right away. I was beginning to think you didn't like me or something!" As she spoke, Tara gave a little shriek of laughter as if the very idea of somebody's not liking her were hysterically funny.

Lexie smiled weakly and crumpled the witch picture into an even smaller ball in her sweaty hand. "Our mail was stuck up inside our mail slot," she explained. "I didn't even get the invitation until a few days ago."

Tara's big eyes got even bigger. "For real? What a bummer! Why, I'd just die if I couldn't get my mail. Particularly my catalogs. You know, my favorite one is—"

A large shadow fell across the desk, and she stopped talking. Both girls turned to look at Mr. Lange, who'd come up behind them and was eavesdropping on their conversation.

"Math homework, Fraulein Nielsen?" he said, folding his beefy arms across his chest. "You have an unusual way of going about it."

Lexie turned redder than ever and gave Mr. Lange a sheepish smile. As soon as the teacher turned his back, she and Tara rolled their eyes at each other. Then Lexie scuttled across the room.

She breathed a long, drawn-out sigh of relief. She vowed to find Cheryl at recess and thank her for trying to find out about Tara's party. Then she made a second vow. In the future, she was going to try not to be so critical of Tara. After all, the other girl couldn't help being rich and pretty and popular and talented. It was probably only natural for her to act a little conceited!

She pulled out her wrinkled wad of math homework papers and spread them out on her desktop. To her amazement, now that she didn't have to worry about Tara and the party and the witch drawing anymore, she was actually able to concentrate on the problems. By the time most of the kids had arrived at school, she was only three assignments behind the rest of the class.

As the minute hand on the clock jerked straight up onto the twelve, Lexie spotted a mistake in her last fraction problem and got out her eraser to correct it. When she did, she noticed the dollar sign she'd gouged into the rubber on Friday. She made a face. She *still* hadn't figured out how to get any presents for her family, and Christmas was only a week away! Even if she did Rent-A-Kid jobs every single day, she wouldn't earn enough money to buy anything decent—particularly if she wanted to contribute toward the cost of Fido's operation.

"What say we read some more of *The Witches* and get this gloomy Monday off to a rip-roaring start?" Mr. Lange was asking.

While the rest of the class clapped and cheered, Lexie drifted backward to Friday afternoon when Mr. Lange had first started reading the book. As she closed her eyes and listened to the teacher's voice, she felt as if she were floating in the air, watching herself sitting at her desk, working away on her witch picture. It had been a really mean and ugly drawing, she realized. But it had been beautifully ugly. And she'd had a lot of fun making it.

That's the way it usually works, Lexie mused to herself. When you have a lot of fun making something, the end result turns out to be pretty good. Most of the time, anyway. Hmmm . . . hmmm . . . whoa!

Lexie's eyes popped open in surprise. From out of the blue, a big jumble of present ideas was crowding its way into her mind! As she swiftly sorted through her confused thoughts, she realized her ideas weren't bad at all. In fact, they were great! And amazing as it seemed, most of the present ideas were for things she already knew how to make!

Her breath came faster. She pulled out a sheet of notebook paper and started scribbling lists and figures. Of course, she told herself as she made several lightning calculations, she'd have to spend some money on materials and ingredients. But, after all, she hadn't told her father she'd give him *all* her Rent-A-Kid money for Fido's vet bill. She was sure he wouldn't mind if she kept at least a few dollars for something as unselfish as Christmas shopping.

She wrote a few more numbers in a column. As she added and then divided, she bit her lip in concentration. All she had to do, she thought, was get a few more snow-shoveling jobs, and she was in the clear. Given the weather lately, that probably wouldn't be a problem. She twisted around and glanced out the classroom window. Sure enough, a few big fat flakes were already floating across the gray sky.

After she got some more money, she went on to herself, she'd have to beg Karen or Daniel to take her to the mall one night this week. But that probably wouldn't be a problem either. Karen loved to shop, and Daniel loved to drive. If either one of them needed any extra convincing, all Lexie had to do was tell them she was searching for their presents!

She glanced down at her totals, nodded, and smiled to herself. Everything added up. Her Christmas list was perfect.

As she put down her pencil, she suddenly noticed how quiet the room had become. With a start, she realized Mr. Lange had stopped reading. She swallowed hard and looked up. The entire class, including the teacher, was staring right at her.

Lexie felt a hot flush rising up from her neck to her face. She cleared her throat, and struggled to think of an explanation for why she hadn't been listening to Mr. Lange read. But before she could open her mouth, the teacher's big face crinkled into a grin.

"I *told* you you'd get into that math homework if you just gave it a chance, didn't I, Mademoiselle Nielsen?"

Lexie nodded and tried to grin back at him. Then she turned her Christmas list facedown on her desk and leaned back to listen to the rest of the story.

Twelve

The next week was a busy one for Lexie. She spent most of her afternoons shoveling snow, walking dogs, watering plants, and picking up mail for people who were away on vacation. When she wasn't doing Rent-A-Kid jobs, she was upstairs in her room with her door closed tight, designing and redesigning her Christmas present plans.

By Wednesday afternoon, Faith was on fire with curiosity. "What are you doing in there, Lexie?" she asked time and again. "Planning the perfect crime? Listing excuses for not doing your homework? Writing the life story of a little twit?"

But nasty as Faith's questions were, Lexie never swallowed the bait and became involved in a fight. "Wait and see," was all she would say. Then she'd give a mysterious little chuckle, carefully calculated to drive her sister even crazier.

On the Thursday night before Christmas, Daniel agreed to give her a ride to the mall. "I have a few different places to go," she told him when they got there. "So why don't you go fondle the soccer balls in the sporting goods shop for a while? I'll meet you later when I'm finished."

Daniel snorted. "Have you been taking bossy lessons from Karen or something?" he asked. But after that, he good-naturedly agreed to meet her at 8:30 by the big Christmas tree in the food court. "Just don't talk to any strangers," he warned.

"I promise!" Lexie called as she hurried off. "At least . . . nobody stranger than you!"

By 8:45 when Lexie finally dashed into the food court, Daniel was just finishing off a triple-scoop chocolate peanut-butter ice cream cone. "You're late," he told her, as he popped the end of the cone into his mouth. "I was about to go to the mall office and report you as a lost toddler."

Lexie stuck out her tongue at him. "I hardly had time

to get everything I needed as it was!" she said breathlessly, gesturing toward her armload of packages. "Can we go home now?"

"Aren't you even going to beg for an ice cream cone?"

"I don't have time. Come *on,* Daniel. Let's go!"

"All *right,*" said her brother. "If you're not whining for an ice cream cone, it must mean you're sick. I'd better get you home fast before you throw up on me!"

Lexie stuck out her tongue again, and the two of them hurried to the nearest exit. As soon as Daniel pulled into the garage, she jumped out of the car, raced back upstairs to her room, and closed the door. She came out only twice—once to steal some tape from Faith's room and once to brush her teeth before bed.

The next day was Friday, the last day of school before Christmas. As 3:00 approached, Lexie felt so jumpy she thought she might not survive until the final bell rang. Of course, she felt the same way every December. But this year, it wasn't only that she was dying for vacation to start. Now she couldn't wait to get home and work on all her projects!

By the afternoon of Christmas Eve she finally had everything completed to her satisfaction. She emerged from her room just in time to accompany her father to Dr. McManus's office to pick up Fido.

When she saw the cat in his carrying box at the animal

hospital, she felt like crying. The once-chubby animal was a pale, weak shadow of his former self. His yellow eyes were huge in his new, thin face.

"He looks so little!" Lexie exclaimed.

"He's lost some weight," Dr. McManus said. "But to tell you the truth, that was probably good for him. He was a little on the obese side when your dad brought him in."

"Too many Kitty Yum-Yums," Lexie explained. "He just can't get enough of them."

Dr. McManus laughed. "Maybe you can help him exercise a little self-control after this." She handed Lexie a sheet of paper. "I've written down instructions for Fido's care at home. You should bring him back for a check-up in a week or so. And don't let him out of the house at night no matter how hard he begs."

Lexie and Mr. Nielsen thanked the doctor and gently carried Fido's box out to the car. When they got home, Lexie made the cat a little bed in a box and put it on his favorite spot on the sunny mat in the back hall. Then she kissed him on his battered head and left him to rest.

When she wandered back into the kitchen, she found her father standing in front of the stove, stirring something in a huge cast-iron pot.

"I'm making our customary feast, Lexie." Mr. Nielsen smacked his lips. "Oyster stew. A Nielsen Christmas Eve tradition."

Lexie groaned and clutched her stomach with both hands. "Yuck! Why can't we start a pizza tradition instead?"

Mr. Nielsen ground some fresh pepper into the stew. "Well, if you don't want any stew, maybe you can find something you like in that Epicurean food box your mother's aunts sent. We thought we'd crack that open tonight."

"Terrific. If I don't want any slimy, mucky oysters, I can fill up on smoked baby clams and Norwegian sardines in mustard sauce!"

Mr. Nielsen shrugged. Then he scooped up a ladleful of soup and tasted it. "Mmmmm," he said blissfully. "Scrumptious. Are you sure you wouldn't like to try some, Lex?"

Lexie made a gagging sound in her throat and backed out of the kitchen. Then she went into the living room to make sure the Christmas tree lights were turned on. In spite of the prospect of a disgusting dinner, she was in her usual happy but slightly nervous Christmas Eve mood. She hummed "Jingle Bells" to herself as she got down on her hands and knees and examined every package under the tree for the fifth time that day.

A few minutes later, her father shouted for everyone to come to the dining room. Lexie was the first one to answer the call. After several more shouts, the whole family arrived. As they all sat down around the table,

Mr. Nielsen gave each one of them a large, steaming serving of stew.

Lexie took one look at the bloblike gray oyster floating in the middle of her bowl and shuddered. Desperately, she cast around for an excuse to leave the table. Just then, Karen spoke up.

"This stew is scrumptious, Daddy! But what about our other Christmas Eve family tradition? We have to listen to some music from your old record collection!"

Lexie leaped to her feet. "I'll go pick something out!" she eagerly volunteered. Before anyone else could say anything, she dashed into the living room and bent down in front of the bookshelves containing her father's beloved but fragile 78-speed records. Some of them were so old they only had grooves on one side of the record.

After a brief search, Lexie found the one she'd always liked best. It was a scratchy recording of some old European church bells playing Christmas carols. Lexie carefully took it out of its yellowing paper envelope, gently placed it onto the turntable, adjusted the speed on the stereo, and turned it on.

The tinny, off-key sound of the bonging bells filled the air and Lexie started back into the dining room. But before she got there, she paused. Without speaking, she stood by the Christmas tree and stared in at the noisy, cheerful table in front of her. As usual, her parents, brother, and sisters were talking too loud, arguing and joking about everything, slurping oyster stew, and only half-listening to the familiar old music.

"It's the old Nielsen jigsaw puzzle again," she said to herself. "Each piece of the family has a life of its own. But we're together forever on Christmas Eve." With a smile, she walked into the dining room and slipped into her place at the table.

Thirteen

On Christmas morning Lexie woke up at 4:00 A.M. She wanted to run around the house and wake up everyone else, but from past experience, she knew the rest of her family would become hysterical if she did. Instead, she crept downstairs and checked on Fido. He was sound asleep in his bed. But when he heard her coming, one of his ears twitched. He lifted his head and softly said, "*Meow.*"

"Merry Christmas to you, too, Fido," Lexie whispered. "Everything sounds so quiet and muffled, I think it must have snowed again last night." She peered out the window in the back door. "Yup, Fido. We got at least six more inches. So much for all my shoveling last week!"

She bent down and picked up the cat's bed. Carefully, she carried the box into the dark living room and tucked it into a warm corner. Then she turned on the Christmas tree lights and curled up on the couch. She pulled an old red and white afghan over herself and breathed in the pungent scent of the balsam needles. Suddenly drowsy, she gazed dreamily at all her favorite old tree ornaments, shimmering and glowing among the dark green branches. In the warm, gentle light from the colored bulbs, she closed her eyes and drifted back to sleep.

Starting at about 6:30, one by one, the rest of her family straggled into the living room. At 7:00, Mrs. Nielsen brought in a pot of hot coffee, a pitcher of orange juice, and a big tray of warm, buttery sticky buns.

"Shall I go whip up a batch of Frank's Famous Scrambled Eggs?" Mr. Nielsen asked. "You know, the ones with parmesan, Monterey Jack, and cottage cheese? They're a tradition, aren't they?"

"Dad*deeee,*" Lexie whined. "The tradition is that we never eat breakfast before we open presents!"

"Well, surely we can make an *eggs*-ception this year, Lexie?"

Her father winked as he spoke, and Lexie grinned at

113

him. "Stop teasing, Daddy. It's *eggs*-tremely *eggs*-as-perating!"

"Stop all these egg jokes!" Karen cried. "They're so corny, they're—"

"*Eggs*-cruciating?" Daniel interrupted. "Don't you think you're being just a little *eggs*-treme in your criticism, Karen?"

"Oh, don't mind her," Lexie giggled. "She's just being *shell*fish because she can't crack any *yolks* of her own!"

"Come on, Daddy," Faith said then. "Stop joking around and let Lexie open her presents."

"Oh, shut up, Faith!" Lexie said. "You know you want to open presents just as much as I do. Stop pretending to be such a big, sophisticated grown-up."

"Now I know I'm home," Karen sighed. "When my adorable little sisters start one of their charming fights on Christmas morning. What *can* we do to help you two learn to get along?"

"You can mind your own business, Karen!" Lexie and Faith spoke the words at the exact same instant, and a few seconds of surprised silence followed their outburst. Then everybody but Karen burst out laughing.

When the family was quiet again, Lexie jumped to her feet. "I don't care what the rest of you are going to do," she announced. "I'm handing out my presents."

She went to the tree and pulled out a pile of brightly

114

wrapped packages. "The first one's for Fido. It's a new cat toy to play with at night because he can't go out anymore." She placed a little round plastic ball in the corner of the cat's bed. "And here's one for you, Mom. And you, Daddy. And you, Karen. And here's yours, Daniel. And last and most definitely least, here's one for you, Faith."

As she spoke, she walked around the living room, handing each person a gift. When she was finished, the only sound in the room was the ripping of wrapping paper. Daniel was the first one to say anything. "Chocolate chip cookies!" he exclaimed. "Oh, boy!"

"I know you asked for raw dough. But I couldn't figure out how to wrap it so I snuck downstairs last night and baked it instead."

"I like it in finished form, too." Daniel took a cookie out of his box and bit into it. "Mmmm. Perfect—half cooked, just the way I like them. Thanks, Lex!"

"I'm not sure I understand what my present is, Lexie," Karen said. She held up an envelope and several pieces of paper. "Are these gift certificates?"

"Sort of. They're work coupons. Each one is for a different job I can do for you when you're home from college. See? There's one for washing the dishes for you on your night. And one for doing your laundry one time. And one for letting you boss me around for a whole morning. Of course, you do that anyway, but . . ."

"I most certainly do not!" Karen interrupted angrily.

"Now sit down on the couch and close your mouth!"

Everyone but Karen laughed again, and she looked around the room in surprise. Then she shook her head and shrugged. "I'm only making *suggestions*," she said with a smile. "Though I'm willing to admit I do over-exceed my authority from time to time. Or *eggs*-ceed, as you dumb clucks would undoubtedly say! But anyway, thank you very much for these, Lex-Lex. They should really come in handy."

"And thank you for mine, Lexie."

The whole family turned to look at Mrs. Nielsen, who was beaming and holding up a small white sign hanging from a brass hook. In neat black letters, Lexie had painted: BARBARA NIELSEN, M.A.

"Daddy told me M.A. stood for 'master of arts,' " Lexie explained.

"It certainly does," Mrs. Nielsen said. She pulled a tissue out of her bathrobe pocket and dabbed at the corner of her eyes. "Believe me, if I ever get around to hanging out a shingle, I'll be proud to use this, Lexie. I know my thesis absorption put a strain on our family's standard patterns of relating, and I just want to thank all of you for being such a strong support system for me during this period of stress." She got to her feet and crossed the room to give Lexie a hug.

"Welcome back from Loony Land, Mom," Lexie said, returning her mother's hug. "I *think*."

Mrs. Nielsen laughed. "Psychology talk aside, honey, you really came up with the perfect present."

"I hate to admit it, but mine's perfect, too."

This time the family turned to look at Faith, who was also holding up a sign on a hook. Hers was big and black. In fat, shiny red letters it said: FAITH'S ROOM. PLEASE KNOCK BEFORE ENTERING. THAT MEANS *YOU*, LEXIE!

Mr. Nielsen chuckled, and Lexie glanced over her shoulder at him. "You haven't even opened your present, Daddy!"

"Well, so I haven't. I was absorbed in watching everyone else." Mr. Nielsen bent over and pulled the paper off the small flat package on his lap. Then he smiled and held up his present for everyone to see. It was a framed photograph of Fido. The cat was lying in his famous "dead dog" position on Lexie's bed.

"That's a wonderful picture of the old boy, Lexie," her father said. "I think I'll take it to work with me and put it on my desk. But now I want to give you something."

He jumped up from his chair, got down on his hands and knees, and started pawing through the packages under the tree. "I have to give you your present right away," he grunted as he searched. "It proves that you and I really did have the occasional meeting of the minds this year. Though I'll have to admit my mind was a bit more absent than usual from time to time."

"Forget it, Daddy."

"I already have!" Mr. Nielsen chuckled from his position under the tree. After a long search, he finally unearthed a small, flat gift almost exactly the same shape and size as the one he'd just opened. He backed out from under the tree, dislodging several ornaments in the process. He handed the package to Lexie, and she ripped it open. Her mouth dropped open and she gasped.

"Well, what in the world is it?" Karen asked.

Lexie held up a picture in a clear plastic frame for everyone to see. It was a photograph of the snowy owl she and her father had discovered on the winter bird count. The camera had caught the bird at the very instant he took off from the middle of the field. His huge wings were just opening up and his talons were only a few inches off the ground. His feathers gleamed snowy white against the pale blue sky. His intelligent yellow eyes stared straight out of the picture.

"Daddy," Lexie said excitedly. "You're sure to win the Audubon prize with this. It's beautiful!"

"Well, if I do say so myself, you're absolutely right. But to tell you the truth, I don't care if I win or not. It was worth it just seeing that magnificent fellow in all his glory."

"But you are going to enter the picture in the contest, aren't you?"

"Of course! But if I win, your name goes on the

plaque right next to mine, Lexie. After all, I couldn't have taken the picture without you. We birders have to stick together!"

Lexie and her father smiled at each other in a moment of perfect communication. Then everyone else started passing around presents, ripping open packages, and exclaiming and thanking each other. Within minutes, the living room rug was covered with boxes, tissue, wrapping paper, and ribbons.

When Lexie had raced through opening her own gifts, she sat back and watched everyone else open theirs. Later, when her father went into the kitchen to make his scrambled eggs, she carried her pile of presents up to her room. She sat down on her bed and began sorting through her new things. Her feet were already sweating inside the huge, fuzzy tiger-foot slippers Daniel had given her. She'd also received several spooky mystery books from Karen, a giant solid chocolate Santa from Faith, and a new ski sweater from her mother. It was pale green with white snowflakes on it, and Lexie had decided it would be the perfect thing to wear to Tara's after-holiday party.

"Not a bad Christmas," she said to herself. "Not bad at all. Now the main thing I have to do is manage to choke down some of Frank's Famously Sickening Scrambled Eggs without throwing up!"

To be on the safe side, she decided to fill up on her chocolate Santa before breakfast. She'd just unwrapped it and bitten off the top of its head when she heard a little noise outside in the hallway. Her door slowly swung open, and Fido staggered into the room. Lexie rushed to pick him up.

"Did you climb all the way up the stairs just to visit me?" she asked as she carefully carried him to her bed. "Was our goofy family getting on your nerves?"

Fido rolled over on his back, stuck his feet up into the air, and purred. Lexie laughed. "That sounds like a 'yes' to me. But weird as they are, Fido, you must admit they're usually somewhere around when you need them. That counts for something, doesn't it? *If* you remember to communicate with them, that is. Communication, I have learned, is the key to survival in this dog-eat-dog world we live in. Or dog-eat-*cat* world, in your case, Fido. As I'm sure Mom's thesis will prove, communication breakdowns are the root cause of Severe Stress Syndrome."

She opened one of her new mysteries and started to read. Just then, the door burst open. "Hey, Lexie," Faith said, coming into the room. "Come and see my door. I hung up my 'Knock Before Entering' sign, and it looks great."

"I can see I'll have to make a sign for myself now," Lexie answered. "Since you never bother knocking on *my* door before you barge in!"

Faith stuck out her tongue. "I can easily solve that

problem by promising never to come in here again. Now hurry on out and see how my sign looks."

Lexie turned over on her back and stifled a yawn. "I'll come see it in a few minutes."

Faith's eyes narrowed. "What are you doing up here all alone on Christmas morning anyway?" she asked.

"I'm enjoying my own company! *And* I'm hoping Daddy won't notice when I don't show up for a helping of those eggs."

Faith laughed. "It won't work," she said. "Believe me. I tried it two years ago, and they hunted me down and force-fed me."

She crossed the room and sat down on the edge of her sister's bed. "Seriously, Lex," she said. "Are you sick or something? I mean, you usually like to be right down in the middle of the action on Christmas, begging for more presents and eating all the candy canes off the tree. Aren't you lonely up here all by yourself?"

"I may be by myself, Faith," Lexie said slowly. "But I'm *not* lonely. Me, Myself, and I are terrific conversationalists, you know!"

Faith stared at her. "Lexie," she said at last, "your rapidly developing case of insanity is really a wonderful stroke of luck for Mom. She can start practicing her new counseling skills right here at home!" She got to her feet. "Now are you coming with me or not?"

"Soon. I said I'd come *soon.*"

Faith shrugged and started toward the door. "Suit yourself. But when you and your split personalities get tired of each other, come back downstairs. If I have to eat some of Daddy's eggs, you do, too—all three of you." She started out into the hall and then stopped. "Besides," she added, "I miss you when you're not around to pick on."

Lexie blinked. By Faith's standards, this was an incredibly warm and friendly thing to say. "Daddy *said* you missed me because you'd moved out of here!" she cried. "Thank you for admitting it, Faith. I miss you, too!"

Faith's face registered surprise, then embarrassment, and then complete horror. Without another word, she ran out of the room, slamming the door behind her.

Lexie listened to her sister's footsteps pounding down the stairs, and she burst out laughing. "Now if that's not communicating," she said, "I don't know what is!"

She rolled over onto her stomach again, and Fido woke up and mewed at her. "Sorry," she told him. She put her mouth close to his ear. "But now that you're awake, I might as well tell you what I just figured out. Being on your own isn't always so bad. And sometimes it can actually be fun!"

Fido mewed again, and Lexie yawned. Then she scratched the cat on top of his head, took another bite of chocolate Santa, and opened up her mystery book again.